ANGEL
on
VACATION

ANGEL
on
VACATION

a novel

DAN YATES

Covenant Communications, Inc.

Cover images ® 2000 PhotoDisc, Inc.

Cover design copyrighted 2000 by Covenant Communications, Inc.

Published by Covenant Communications, Inc.
American Fork, Utah

Printed in the United States of America
First Printing: April 2000

07 06 05 04 03 02 01 00   10 9 8 7 6 5 4 3 2 1

ISBN 1-57734-645-9

PROLOGUE

Samantha had come a long way since her days in the mortal world, where she found herself being courted by a ghost. What choice did poor Jason have but to court her as a ghost—or perhaps a better word would be angel? Because of a typo on the contract linking Jason's destiny with Samantha's, Jason was born thirty years too soon. But in the end, Jason was able to set destiny straight through his relentless refusal to let Samantha slip through his ghostly fingers. Once he convinced her she was in love with him, it was a simple matter to set things right when the higher authorities approved Samantha to cross over and be with Jason on his side of forever.

Samantha soon learned that being an angel wasn't all that bad. In fact, it was downright exciting. Being a dyed-in-the-wool Cupid's helper at heart, she soon found her niche in this new dimension. She also met Gus, the Special Conditions Coordinator responsible for the typo. Special Conditions Coordinators deal mainly with forever contracts between individuals on the mortal side of the line, and Samantha was actually able to assist Gus with a few of his cases, starting with her own former fiancé. Although Gus had been reluctant to let her help at first, Samantha had become friends with Maggie, his personal secretary, and that had made all the difference.

As for Jason? Well, at first Jason just went along with the idea to pacify Samantha. But little by little, the fun of working alongside Samantha on these cases won him over. Not that he ever really admitted to his change of heart, but it was there, nonetheless.

Samantha's big break came when Gus and Maggie were moved upstairs to new, higher positions as Special Conditions Coordinators over an entire universe. Samantha and Jason were chosen to replace Gus, working as partners. And the best part was that they were moved up to second-level angels in order to qualify. Being moved from a first-level angel to a second-level angel in so short a time on the far side of forever was rare. Second-level angels carried a lot more responsibility. They had the authority to make higher-level decisions and could do many things a first-level angel couldn't. Samantha loved her new job. Jason was apprehensive at first—but it grew on him in time.

One of the most satisfying assignments Samantha experienced in her first year as Special Conditions Coordinator was working with her own brother, Michael. When she was first given the assignment to secure a forever contract between Michael and Jenice Anderson, Samantha didn't like Jenice at all. But once the feisty angel got to know Michael's true love better, she was in Jenice's corner all the way.

The assignment wasn't actually in the completed file yet, but it was close now. Michael and Jenice's wedding was less than a month away. And that is where our story picks up.

CHAPTER 1

As Jenice Anderson gazed at the man seated across the table from her, she sighed to herself. *Mrs. Michael Allen.* The name rippled freely through the chambers of her mind. It was such a splendid name, and yet she felt a nervous chill as she realized it would be hers in less than a month. Over and over again she had asked herself why—why couldn't she just accept the fact she would be Michael's wife without these haunting doubts stabbing constantly at her heart? Why indeed? The answer was obvious. Because she was Jenice Anderson, and Jenice Anderson was not like most women. Jenice loved adventure, and in the past, thoughts of marriage had always been accompanied by the threat of having to sacrifice so many of her dreams, which was something, in her opinion, she had observed her own mother do.

There was no question that Jenice was in love with Michael. She cringed to think how close she had come to losing him. But that was all in the past. Nothing would stand in her way of becoming his wife now, not even her worries over giving up a life of adventure— although Michael had promised to honor her longing for adventure after they were married. And Michael was a lover of adventure himself. So why was she worried? Because she was Jenice Anderson, that's why.

Her thoughts were interrupted when Michael spoke. "How's your steak?" he asked. "Done enough to suit you?"

Jenice smiled innocently at him. It was no secret she liked her steak cooked to the point it was nearly burnt. What could she say? It was just the way she had learned to eat steak as a girl. Michael, on the other hand, liked his steak so rare she often wondered if it had been put over the fire at all. "My steak is perfect," she responded, "but I could have sworn I heard yours say 'moo' on your first bite."

"Very funny, Jenice Anderson," Michael grinned. "At least mine tastes like a fine steak should. You might as well bite into a chunk of charcoal."

"Hey, would you look at this?" Jenice exclaimed. "We're not even married yet, and we're already having our first argument."

"At least we both agree where to find the best steak," he observed. "You didn't give me the slightest hassle when I suggested a poolside table at the Hunter's Cottage."

"Why would I object to the Hunter's Cottage?" she responded with a teasing smile. "I've loved the food in this place ever since Bruce Vincent first brought me here. In fact, it was at this very table that Bruce proposed to me."

"Was not!" Michael snapped.

"Was too!" she shot right back.

"This very table we're sitting at right now?"

Jenice nodded.

Michael's face became expressionless, and Jenice fought to keep her own face straight, but it was no use. She broke out laughing. "But you know I gave his ring back, big guy. You're the only one who's ever managed to get a serious 'yes' out of me."

Michael stared at her for a long moment. At last, he spoke. "So, Miss Anderson, are you having second thoughts about putting on that white dress and signing a forever contract with this freelance artist who thinks you like your steak overcooked?"

Jenice drew a slow deliberate breath. "I'd be lying if I said I wasn't nervous," she admitted.

"Oh?" Michael came back, one eyebrow arched. "You are having second thoughts, then?"

"I didn't say I was having second thoughts," Jenice clarified. "I only said I was nervous. There's no way I'd back out of marrying you, Michael Allen." Her teasing smile returned. "Besides, do you know what that sister of yours would do to me if I tried?"

"Now there's a confidence-builder if I ever heard one," Michael laughed. "You're marrying me because you're afraid of what Sam will do if you don't."

"Yes," she agreed. "That's true. I'm afraid of your sister—plus I'm madly in love with you to the point that I can't imagine living another day without you in my life."

Michael smiled warmly. "It's still hard for you to say you love me, isn't it?"

"Don't be mad at me, Michael," Jenice pleaded. "But, yes, it is hard. You know it's always been hard for me to say that to a man. Any man—even my father." Her eyes softened. "If it's any consolation, it is getting easier for me to tell you."

"I'll take what I can get," he chuckled. "So tell me, Jenice. Where do you want to go on your honeymoon? Hawaii? Tahiti? Novosibirsk, Russia?"

"Novosibirsk, Russia?" Jenice stared at him. "What, pray tell, is in Novosibirsk, Russia, that I could possibly be interested in?"

"I don't know. I've never been there," he laughed. "There's no telling what I've missed in my life. And what *we'll* miss," he said, "if we don't spend our honeymoon there."

Jenice shook her head firmly. "I'm sorry, Mr. Allen, but Novosibirsk, Russia, is out. If you want to honeymoon there, you'll have to do it without me."

Michael shrugged. "Okay, Russia is out. So let's go to Miami, Florida."

"What?!" Jenice choked. "Miami, Florida? I'm a girl who loves adventure, Michael, and I'm not talking the sort of adventure you can have at Disney World."

"No, but the sort of adventure I have in mind for Miami is a little more exciting than Disney World. Let me give you a hint. If it be adventure ye be seekin', lassie, then adventure ye'll be havin', says I."

"The captain's sunken gold?" Jenice asked. "You want to go after it on our honeymoon?"

"And why not?" Michael retorted. "You love adventure, I love adventure, what greater adventure can you name than searching the floor of the Atlantic for sunken gold?"

Jenice considered it. She was aware, naturally, that Michael had Captain Blake's map showing the location of the sunken treasure, she'd just never given much thought about the "if" and "when" they might go looking for it. That was a crazy idea, spending a honeymoon looking for sunken gold. Even Jenice Anderson wouldn't go that far just for the sake of an adventure. Or would she? As Michael had so aptly put it, "Why not?"

"It is a tempting thought at that," she admitted. "But . . ."

"But what, Jenice Anderson?"

"But it's a little out of our reach at the moment, Michael. Money-wise, I mean. We'd have to have a boat, diving equipment, a place to stay . . . That all takes money, and money is something we're a little short of right now, in case you've forgotten."

From the playful look on Michael's face, Jenice knew she was missing something—she had no idea what. But, she was about to find out. "What would you say if I told you I just sold some paintings?" he asked. "Sold them for enough to pay for a dozen excursions in quest of the captain's gold."

"What paintings?" she asked. "I know you've been working on one lately, but I also know it's not finished."

His next question caught her completely by surprise. She had no idea what he was getting at. "Ever hear of Welmington Park?" he asked.

"Sure I've heard of Welmington Park. I did a story on it for my newspaper. It was when they dug up the park in preparation for building a high-rise business complex in its place. Made a lot of people unhappy, let me tell you. Welmington Park had been there for the public to enjoy for more than a hundred years. Then some business tycoon comes up with a scheme to do away with it. It's a wonder someone didn't lynch the man." Jenice stopped to search the expression on Michael's face. "What does Welmington Park have to do with you selling some paintings?"

"It has everything to do with it," Michael answered. "Eight years ago I did a series of paintings in the park. I captured the children's playground, the old waterwheel, the boathouse, the famous old mulberry tree, a sunset over the lake, a boy flying his kite in the September wind, and a rainy summer's afternoon. Six of them altogether."

Jenice was startled. "Huh? I never saw those paintings. Where have you kept them hidden all these years?"

Seeing that he had caught his fiancée off-guard, Michael smiled. "I had them hanging in the entertainment room of my Uncle Mac's place until he died a year or so back."

"Your Uncle Mac?" Jenice asked curiously. "I don't remember your ever mentioning you had an uncle."

"People knew him as J.T. MacGregor," Michael said, watching her face for some sign of recognition.

Jenice's face lit up. "That's right. He was your uncle, wasn't he? I interviewed him once. He had just made a big donation to the cancer fund as a memorial to his wife."

Michael nodded. "Yeah, Uncle Mac always was generous to the cancer fund. Aunt Katherine died of cancer, you know. It almost did Uncle Mac in. He was never the same."

Jenice's face was filled with sympathy. "I knew about your aunt. I learned it from J.T. in the interview."

"When Uncle Mac died, my cousins Lisa and Julie sold his old house," Michael continued. "After that, I sealed up my paintings and stored them in a closet at Lisa's house. A couple of weeks ago, I got a call from the museum where I used to work. They informed me they were doing an art display and wanted to know if I had any paintings I might loan them. So I got the paintings back from Lisa and loaned them to the museum."

"So the museum bought your paintings?" Jenice guessed.

Michael grinned. "No, not the museum. Randolph Johnson bought them."

"Randolph Johnson? The billionaire Randolph Johnson?"

"One and the same. Randolph happened to spot my paintings at the museum. It seems that he grew up in a house across the street from Welmington Park although in those days he was far from wealthy. His family was quite poor, in fact. When he saw my paintings, he fell in love with them. Offered me $100,000."

Jenice gasped. "You sold the six paintings for $100,000?"

Michael's eyes gleamed with mischief. "No, I sold them for $100,000 *each*. There's nothing cheap about Randolph Johnson. He gave me $600,000 and never batted an eye."

While Jenice stared, gaping, at Michael, he nonchalantly cut off a corner of steak and placed it in his mouth, acting as if he sold paintings for a half a million dollars every day of the week.

"Are you lying to me, Michael Allen?!" Jenice half shouted. "Because if you are, I don't think it's one bit funny."

Michael made her wait while he slowly finished chewing. "I've never lied to you in my life," he said without looking up from his plate. "Why would I start now?"

Now it was Jenice's turn to grow silent. For the next several minutes, the two of them continued their meal with not a word spoken. Jenice wiped her lips with her napkin, then sat just looking at Michael for several more seconds. Then she resolutely raised a finger and waved it toward him. "You're telling me you have $600,000 in a savings account?" she pressed.

Still, he didn't look up. "Yep."

"And you're telling me I can go anywhere I want to go on my honeymoon?"

"Yep."

"Okay," Jenice said, nodding. "That's what I want to do. I want to explore the floor of the Atlantic Ocean for the captain's gold."

Lifting his napkin to his mouth, Michael dabbed at the corners and looked up until his eyes met those of his fiancée. "Done," he said.

All at once a tremendous excitement hit her. She had a sudden urge to stand and shout in sheer delight. It was all she could do to restrain herself. Exploring the floor of the Atlantic?! Talk about an adventure! She drew a deep breath and turned her attention back to Michael. "I don't want to wait!" she blurted out.

"Wh—what?" he stammered. "We have to wait, Jenice. The wedding plans are already cast in stone."

"That's not what I mean," she said urgently. "I know we can't move the wedding up. But I don't want to wait for my adventure. Let's go tomorrow. Why do we have to wait until we're married?"

"Well . . ." Michael said slowly. "Honeymoons always seem to come after the marriage. It's just the way things are done."

"Then we won't call it a honeymoon. We'll just call it . . ." She waved both hands energetically, looking for the right word, "uh . . . a pre-wedding vacation. What the heck, we can always go to Novosibirsk, Russia, for our actual honeymoon."

"But—what about your job at the newspaper? George Glaser won't take lightly to your taking time off now, and then again in a month for the honeymoon."

"I can handle George Glaser," Jenice insisted. "I've never met an editor yet I couldn't handle. I'll have him eating out of my hand. When he thinks the *Morning Municipal* will get the scoop on the discovery of a sunken treasure the size of Captain Blake's, I'm betting he'll offer to pay all the expenses. Think of it, Michael. That just means more of the $600,000 we can keep."

Michael dropped the napkin back to his lap. "You're serious about this, aren't you?" he asked.

"I am," she said solemnly.

Michael placed an elbow on the table and rested his chin on his hand. "All right," he said after a moment or two. "We'll go tomorrow. What the heck, why put off a good adventure?"

Jenice was around the table in two bounds. She planted a kiss on his lips. "Thank you, Michael," she said. "You promised if I married you I wouldn't have to give up my dreams, and you're proving it to me."

"Jenice," Michael said, rolling his eyes. "Everyone's looking at us."

"Oh yeah, they are, aren't they?" she grinned. "Might as well give them something to see." She slid onto his lap and kissed him again.

* * *

At a table on the far side of the patio, a man sat alone in the shadows. An odd grin twisted his lips as he stared at these two happy lovers. "You've still got it, old man," he said to himself. "Tapping the telephone lines of these two was rewarding enough. But planting a bug in the lady's purse was a stroke of genius." A dark laugh escaped his lips. "I know more about the two of you than you know about yourselves. Going to Miami tomorrow, are we? That's fine. That's just fine. And when you go after the captain's gold, I'll be there with the welcome wagon just for you. Oh, and about that honeymoon next month—I doubt you'll be troubled with picking a spot for it. I doubt you'll be troubled at all."

CHAPTER 2

Samantha and Jason stood outside their own office as Samantha let her fingers glide smoothly over the letters on the closed door. "Jason and Samantha Hackett, Special Conditions Coordinators," she said, dreamily reading the words engraved there. "Does that sound neat, or what?"

Jason shrugged. "I don't know. I guess it sounds okay. All right, I admit it. I like the job better now than when I first inherited it. Maybe it's not growing on me as fast as you'd like it to, Sam, but it is growing on me."

Samantha lowered her hand and turned to face Jason. "I personally think it's pretty darn neat that we've been on this side of forever barely two mortal years, and we're already set up with our own office where we can help people improve their lives."

Jason grinned. "By improve people's lives, I assume you mean making them the target of your Cupid's arrows."

"That's what Special Conditions Coordinators are supposed to do, in case you haven't read the fine print at the bottom of your job description," Samantha huffed. "And what's wrong with adding a little romance to someone's life, anyway? If it were left up to you, all we'd ever do is help someone learn how to cook a better steak."

"Hey, I happen to love cooking. What's so bad about that?"

Samantha shook her head. "Now there's an understatement if ever I heard one. I'd say you pretty well drove that point home earlier tonight, wouldn't you? I mean, how many men would take their wife to the greatest dining house on this side of the galaxy and then leave her sitting alone while he went into the kitchen to cook up their dinner?"

"This is our anniversary, Sam. We deserve the best, and if that requires that I cook the meal, well, so be it. You're not complaining about the dinner I fixed, are you?"

"No, Jason," Samantha relented. "I'm not complaining about the food. And it was certainly romantic, dining in the fabulous Paradise Palace, I'll give you that."

Jason nodded. "And I'll give you this, Mrs. Hackett. Being a Special Conditions Coordinator isn't all bad—we do get to help people." He winked and added, "And doing it with you does add a measure of fun to the game."

"You'd better think that way," Samantha said with a pinch to his cheek. Then looking back at the still unopened door to their office, she paused. "Why did Gus ask you to bring me by the office after we finished dinner tonight?" she asked. "Is he going to meet us here, or what?"

Jason looked confused. "Gus didn't say anything to me, Sam. I thought Maggie had spoken to you about us stopping by the office."

"What?" Samantha laughed. "Maggie didn't say a word to me. Where did you ever get an idea like that?"

"When I was in the kitchen, fixing dinner, one of the chefs told me that Maggie had stopped by your table and asked us to meet her here at the office after dinner," Jason explained. "Are you saying that isn't what happened?"

Samantha's eyes narrowed. "Something's fishy here, Jason. I was sent word while you were in the kitchen that Gus had contacted you about us stopping by the office."

Samantha and Jason looked first at each other, then at the office door. "Someone is playing games with us, Sam," Jason observed. "What do you suppose is waiting for us behind this office door?"

Samantha shrugged. "Beats me, Jason. But there's only one way to find out."

Jason cautiously reached for the knob and gave it a twist, then pushed the door open a crack. To their surprise, the office was completely dark. But it shouldn't have been dark, since lights never go out in a celestial office.

"What do you make of it, Sam?" Jason asked.

Samantha reached out and pushed the door the rest of the way open. "I don't know, Jason. But, being second-level angels, we should be able to bring the lights back on with a simple snap of our fingers. Do you want to take care of it, or shall I?"

Jason snapped his fingers. To the complete surprise of both, nothing happened. "I don't get it, Sam," he said, barely able to see her in the dark. "I did it exactly like we were taught in Special Conditions Coordinator School. Why didn't the lights come on?"

"Let me try," Samantha suggested. Stepping into the room, she snapped her fingers. Still no lights. "Someone is obviously overriding us, Jason. What do you say we try combining our efforts? On the count of three, okay?"

They moved a step farther into the room. Samantha started the count. One—two . . . As she reached three, they snapped their fingers simultaneously. Instantly, the room filled with light and both were stunned to find themselves looking into the smiling faces of a dozen or more people. "HAPPY ANNIVERSARY, SAM!" the crowd shouted in unison. "HAPPY ANNIVERSARY, JASON! WE LOVE YOU!!!"

Samantha blinked. She couldn't believe her eyes. Maggie and her husband, Alvin, were there, and so were Gus and Joan. There was Captain Blake with his beloved Angela Marie, and Uncle Mac, and Aunt Katherine, and . . .

Samantha broke into tears as she spotted Grandmother and Grandfather Collens. It was so strange seeing her own grandparents looking no more than twenty to twenty-five years old. The part about everyone looking young on this side of forever was something Samantha was still trying to get used to.

"You all remembered," Samantha sobbed, one hand covering her mouth. "This is wonderful. I thought you'd forgotten."

"Forget your anniversary?" Maggie laughed. "Never! I'm sorry we couldn't let you bake your own anniversary cake, Jason, but you'll just have to settle for this one. We had it shipped in from the Sugar Belt Galaxy, and you of all people should know their reputation when it comes to desserts. Especially baked desserts."

Samantha's attention was directed to a table in the middle of the room with a gorgeous cake decorating the center of it. She had to laugh when she saw that on the cake was a replica of Jason and herself in the center of a huge heart with a Cupid's arrow through it.

"This is all so wonderful," Samantha said, brushing a finger past the corner of her eye. "Thank you. Thank you all so very much."

"'Tis nothing more than ye deserves, lassie," Captain Blake spoke up, "and Jason as well, says I. Although I be thinkin' the cake might have been better in the shape of a three-mast sailin' vessel movin' through the white crests of some balmy ocean waves."

Samantha had to smile at the captain. She had grown quite fond of him since meeting him on the Caribbean island where he had remained for some three hundred years. When his ship had gone down in a storm, he had been stranded on the island. He'd managed to stay alive until he'd fallen into a deep cave, and even then he'd refused to cross the line to the other side of forever until he felt his final mission in the mortal world was complete.

His mission was to get the map showing the location of his sunken ship—with its cargo of gold—into the hands of a living descendent of Oscar Welborn, the man whose gold he had been carrying on his final voyage. The captain had promised to deliver the gold to Oscar's family in the new world, but when the captain's ship sank in a storm, the gold never made it to its destination.

Ultimately it had been Samantha who had helped the captain accomplish his mission, and the captain had, at last, crossed over to the other side. Once there, he had helped Samantha and Jason in some of their assignments, and as fate would have it, the only living descendent of Oscar Welborn ended up being none other than Michael Allen, Samantha's own brother.

"Don't be payin' one bit of attention to this crusty old sea captain," Angela Marie Blake said, grabbing her husband by the arm and pulling him back a step. "The cake be lovely just the way it be. And them be *me* words."

Jason rubbed his chin. "I have to admit, the cake does look good. But the real proof is in the tasting. I've heard about the chefs from the Sugar Belt Galaxy ever since I first came here. Let's just see if they're as good as they're cracked up to be."

"Here ya go, Jase," Gus said, handing Jason a knife. "Since you're the chef among us, it's only fittin' you do the honors of cuttin' yer own cake."

"Hold on, Gus," Maggie broke in. "We'll cut the cake when the time comes. First we have a little something here for the honored couple." Maggie handed an envelope to Samantha.

Samantha took the envelope curiously. "What is it, Maggie?" she asked.

"It's your anniversary present, Sam," Maggie beamed, stepping forward and placing a lei, first around Samantha's neck and then another around Jason's. "A two-week vacation in the exotic South Celestial Islanders Galaxy, where they have a little of everything. Mountains so scenic no artist's brush can do them justice, crystal-blue oceans for snorkeling among paradisiacal sea coral deposited eternities ago, meadows of grass and flowers beyond description where you can enjoy horseback riding, and beaches with golden sand where you can relax under the warmth of the Seven Sister Suns."

"The South Celestial Islanders Galaxy?" Jason broke in excitedly. "Hey! I've got friend from that galaxy! His name's Daniel Adams and he's the head chef in a celestial dinning room called the Golden Star. When Sam and I were attending Special Conditions Coordinator School, the food was catered by the Golden Star. I got to know Daniel quite well. We had great times trading recipes."

Maggie's smile grew wider. "All the more reason you'll want to vacation there, Jason. And for you, Sam, they have some quaint little sea village shops like you've only dreamed of until now. You have my word, this will be a vacation neither of you will ever forget. And it's all because of your Uncle Mac. He conceived the idea, and he made all the arrangements."

"A two-week dream vacation?" Samantha asked, unbelieving. "And it was your doing, Uncle Mac?" She glanced at her uncle with a laugh. "It sure didn't take long for you to learn your way around on this side, did it?"

"No sense letting moss grow under your feet," he allowed. "Not even celestial moss. Hard as it is for me to admit, I owe you big time, Sam, after what you did for the girls and me."

Well did Samantha remember locking horns with Uncle Mac while he was still on the mortal side. Somehow he had gotten it into his head that his girls were going to marry for money, not something as unreliable as love, and Samantha had had to intervene on behalf of her two cousins, Lisa and Julie. Samantha had managed to change his mind, and both of his daughters had married the men of their dreams. And Uncle Mac? He was called home to this side of forever where he could be with his beloved Katherine. Everything had worked out well, thanks to Samantha never giving up on him.

Samantha looked at the envelope in her hand. "Thank you, Uncle Mac. And thanks to the rest of you, too. It was a wonderful thought. But—I'm just not sure we can be spared out of the office right now."

"What?" Jason objected. "No way are we turning this down, Sam. Not with all those exotic kitchens out there awaiting my inspection, we're not."

"I didn't say we had to turn it down, Jason. I only said we might have to postpone the trip until a time when we're not so stacked up at the office."

"Hogwash!" J.T. spit out. "You're beginning to sound just like me, when I was back in my mortal state. Thought the whole world needed my input just to get the sun up in the morning. Ha, I was a fool. Things have run just fine with me on this side, and even for those two daughters of mine who I thought needed me so badly. Look at the facts, Sam. The office will get by just fine without you for a couple of weeks."

"J.T. is right, Sam," Maggie agreed, smiling. "Gus and I don't mind a bit doing double duty for a couple of weeks. And the good captain will be here to help if we need him. He's still on assignment to keep a close check on Howard Placard, where you placed him on that Caribbean island."

Ah, yes, Howard Placard. Howard had been part of another one of Samantha's assignments. Actually, Samantha's assignment had been to work with two people whose lives Howard had almost ruined, but in the process she had seen something in the man no one else could see. When he was faced with prison for his financial dealings, she had banned him instead to a tiny island in the Caribbean. There she intended him to stay until she could get back to him. Until that time, she had placed Captain Blake in charge of looking after Howard.

"Aye, lassie," Captain Blake went on to say. "Maggie be speakin' the truth. Ye can depend on the captain to keep things in order here while ye be about yer journey across the skies, says I."

"Well I—" Samantha began.

"Well I nothing, Sam," Jason cut in. "You're outnumbered this time. Come on, let's get this cake cut. I'm dying to see just how good those guys at the Sugar Belt Galaxy really are."

CHAPTER 3

Standing in the hallway, Stuart Fox stared at the numbers on the hotel room door, 560, wondering why he had been invited here. Stuart was confident that the reason had something to do with money, and he assumed from the way the stranger had put it—it was about *big* money. Stuart drew a breath and rapped on the door. Seconds later, it opened, and he found himself looking into the face of a man who appeared to be in his early to mid-thirties. Then Stuart did a double take. The face didn't fit the image he had drawn in his mind when he spoke earlier with this man over the phone. He had pictured a more rugged character, one with danger written into his features.

"Stuart Fox, I presume," the stranger said.

When Stuart answered in the affirmative, the man stepped to one side. "Please, come in," he invited Stuart.

Entering the room, Stuart followed the man to a small table with two chairs that stood in one corner. "Would you like something to drink?" the man asked, before either sat down.

"No," Stuart responded. "I came here to talk. Let's get on with it."

The two men sat down. "You mentioned something about a sunken treasure off the coast of Saint Thomas Island on the phone," Stuart began. "Gold, you said."

The man nodded. "That's right. A fortune in gold. Just waiting to be scooped off the ocean floor."

"And you know where this treasure lies?" Stuart quizzed through narrowed eyes.

"No. Not yet, anyway. There's a map showing the exact location of the treasure. I intend to have that map, but I need some help in obtaining it. And I'll need help retrieving the gold once it's found. That's where you come in, Fox. I understand you're a man of enterprise, even when that enterprise doesn't hold the blessing of local law authorities."

"I've been known to look the other way at times," Stuart said curtly. "Exactly what is it you need from me?"

"The first thing I need is a boat and a crew that can be trusted. You come highly recommended, Fox. I hear you're capable of procuring just about anyone or anything needed for a job."

Stuart nodded crisply. "That's right. I can provide whatever you need and whoever you need at a moment's notice. Tell me more."

The stranger relaxed. "Good," he said. "We both stand to make a lot of money from this little undertaking. The map is in the hands of a Michael Allen. Michael along with his girlfriend, Jenice Anderson, are here in Miami now. They're making arrangements for a preliminary dive, just to be sure the gold is actually there."

"I see," Stuart responded with a sly smile. "And you want me and my men to assist them in their quest, is that it?"

The stranger looked directly into Stuart's eyes. "I want it understood up front—no one gets hurt. All I want is the location of the gold. Mr. Allen and the woman have rented a boat and plan on making the dive tomorrow morning. I've already covered all the preliminaries. I have a tracking device aboard their boat, so finding them should be easy. Hopefully, you can find them while they're in the water looking for the gold. If not, then we'll hope they have a map in their possession. Are you with me so far?"

"I'm with you." Stuart nodded.

"All right, now here's the deal. If anything goes wrong—if you don't catch the pair at the actual sight of their dive, or if you end up without a map—here's how I want it handled. Get rid of Mr. Allen. I don't want him hurt, just disable his boat or whatever else you can come up with to get the task done. Bring the woman in. If it comes down to prying the location of the map out of someone, the woman is the better choice. I've done my homework on her, and I know how to get her to tell us where the map is. Does this all sound agreeable to you, Mr. Fox?"

Stuart didn't like the part about no one being hurt. It was his policy to leave no witnesses. But what the stranger didn't know wouldn't hurt the operation in the end. "Agreed," he said easily.

"And you can have a boat with a crew ready by tomorrow morning?"

"I already have some men in mind. And believe me, these men are perfect for the job. They own a yacht, and they're well geared for everything you indicate we need." What Stuart didn't mention was that these men were both known drug dealers. *So what?* Stuart figured. They owned the fastest yacht around and had a half dozen other cutthroats working with them. No question about it, they would be perfect for this operation.

"Good," the man said. "Now let's talk percentages. The way I see it, I take seventy percent. The rest you're free to split any way you see fit."

Stuart tapped the table with his fingers. "You want seventy percent for yourself?" he quizzed. "And you expect the rest of us to divvy up thirty percent? Sounds a little lopsided, if you ask me, friend. I'll just see myself to the door."

"No, wait!" the man said as Stuart rose from his chair. "We'll make it a sixty-forty split. We're talking BIG bucks here. The gold is on a ship that went down on its way to the new world more than three hundred years ago. According to my sources, there's a fortune there just waiting to be grabbed."

Stuart thought a moment. "We split fifty-fifty or no deal," he said flatly. "That gives you a full fifty percent all for yourself. I'll need to pay the crew out of my share."

"All right," the man agreed finally. "Fifty-fifty. I can live with that."

Stuart stood looking at him for several seconds. "You have me at a disadvantage here, mister. I prefer knowing the name of those I do business with."

The man nodded, then handed Stuart one of his business cards. "It's a pleasure doing business with you, Fox. Let's hope we both end up so well off from this endeavor that neither of us will ever have to work again."

CHAPTER 4

Jenice glanced through her diver's mask at the figure hovering in the icy waters just to her left. Even in a rubber wet suit, at the bottom of the Atlantic Ocean, and with a stream of air bubbles flowing upward past his thick, nearly white blond hair, Michael Allen was the handsomest man she had ever laid eyes on. She couldn't believe how close she had come to losing him forever. If it hadn't been for the intervention of his sister, Sam, angel that she was, Jenice would be off chasing some rainbow with Roy Jenkins about now. Despite her brief engagement to a fellow reporter, she had known she didn't love him. How thankful she was that she was here with Michael where she belonged.

Jenice's eyes shifted from Michael to the large wooden chest lying half buried in the silky sand of the ocean floor. A chest that had lain untouched since Captain Horatio Symington Blake's cutter fell victim to a South Atlantic storm more than three hundred years earlier. As Jenice watched Michael reach out and run his hand over the hard wooden surface, she could almost feel the rough texture beneath her fingers. She marveled at its condition after all these years in the cold, salty waters. The entire wreckage was in amazing condition considering the elements it had been subjected to. Could the angels have had something to do with it being preserved, or were the craftsmen of Captain Blake's day well versed in how to prepare their hardwood creations for withstanding the elements? She could only wonder.

Removing a small crowbar from his utility belt, Michael slid it through the opening of the lock affixed to the chest. One quick yank and the lock flew open. Michael reached for the lid but paused to glance back at Jenice. Their eyes met and she gave a brisk nod indicating for him to open the chest. He drew a deep breath and exhaled in a flutter of air bubbles boiling upward toward the ocean's surface. Would the gold be there? she wondered. Captain Blake had promised it would, and Captain Blake was known for keeping his word.

She watched as Michael pulled open the lid, giving her a front-row look at the contents inside the chest. Never in her wildest dreams could she have envisioned such a sight. She moved in closer, brushing against Michael as the two of them stared in awe at the shiny gold bars and coins filling the old chest to nearly overflowing. A smile crossed Jenice's lips as she watched Michael throw up both hands in a show of jubilation. He pulled her into a hug and they both laughed within their masks.

Then, kneeling next to the open chest, Michael removed a dozen coins and dropped them into a leather pouch attached to his utility belt. After one last lingering look, he closed the lid. Taking Jenice by the hand, he gave a hard squeeze, and together they made their way toward the surface where they scrambled back into their waiting boat.

"Captain Blake was telling the truth, Michael!" Jenice shouted, pulling off her mask. "It's there! Have you ever seen such a sight in your life?"

"Not even close," Michael laughed, pulling out the twelve coins for a closer look. "You wanted an adventure, Jenice. How does this stack up?"

She smiled, looking over his shoulder at the coins in his hand. "You know what I think," she said. "I think it was almost too easy. I mean, one dive and we're there. I almost wish it could have been a little harder. Just like that, the adventure is over."

"What do you mean the adventure is over?" Michael asked. "Half the fun will be in retrieving the gold off the ocean floor. But that can wait until after the wedding. Agreed?"

"Agreed," she nodded.

Michael put the coins back in the pouch and tossed it on top of the boat's control panel. With his hands free, he pulled Jenice to him in a very meaningful kiss. Backing away only inches, he asked, "How does it feel to be kissing a rich man, Miss Anderson?"

Jenice lay her head on his shoulder and snuggled close. "About the same as marrying one, I suppose."

"Yeah," Michael laughed. "That does bring up a question, doesn't it? Are you marrying me for who I am or for my money?"

Jenice laughed. "Rich, poor, who cares? If you want to know the real reason I'm marrying you instead of Bruce Vincent or Roy Jenkins, just ask. I'll be more than happy to tell you."

"Okay, I'm listening. What is the real reason, lady? It had better be a good one or I might just have to toss you overboard."

"Ha!" she shot back. "You make threats like that to a woman holding a black belt in karate? You are a brave one, Michael Allen—either that or stupid."

"Humph. Let's leave it at brave," Michael said dryly. "I think I like that better. So—what's this mysterious reason you're harboring for marrying me instead of the others?"

"Think about it, Michael," she teased. "I could have become Jenice Jenkins, or at one time I could have become Jenice Vincent. If I were Jenice Jenkins, everyone would call me J.J. That, I would hate with a passion. And if my last name were Vincent, it would put me at the back of any list arranged in alphabetical order. Not a good thing for an aggressive reporter like myself. With you, I practically stay right where I am now. Jenice Anderson. Jenice Allen. I keep my time-honored initials and actually move up a notch in the alphabet. Why else would I marry you, Michael? Answer me that one if you can!"

"Makes sense to me," Michael grinned. "And while you're at it, my name gives you another advantage—Allen is shorter than Anderson. It'll be easier for you to remember how to spell your own last name. That should be important to an aggressive reporter like yourself."

Jenice stepped backward for greater momentum as she shoved a fist into Michael's shoulder. "I'll have you know I can outspell you any day of the week," she huffed. "I'm a reporter and reporters have to be good spellers. Go ahead, give me a word. Any word you can think of. And don't think you have to go easy on me either, because I won't go easy on you when my turn comes. Go on, give me a word."

Michael looked alarmed. "Hey, I was joking, okay? You don't have to prove anything to me."

"Not okay. You hinted that I can't spell. Now give me a word. And make it your best shot," Jenice insisted.

"A word," Michael said, raising his eyes in thought. "Okay, let's see. How about—psychedelic?"

"Psychedelic?" she echoed. "Where did you ever come up with a word like 'psychedelic'? That's not even a word a reporter would ever use."

"It is, too," Michael defended himself. "I've seen lots of articles with the word 'psychedelic' in them."

"Ha! Give me one example!"

Michael just laughed and shook his head. "You're crazy, you know that, Jenice?"

"Sure I'm crazy. You knew that before you fell in love with me. If you wanted a stay-at-home, sanity-loving sort of wife, you'd have written me off years ago. And you know it, don't you?"

Michael punched Jenice's jaw playfully. "All I said is you're crazy. I never said I didn't like you that way."

"Yeah, well right now I'm just crazy enough to want a change of clothes. This wet suit is darned uncomfortable. Wait here okay, big guy? I'll be right back." Jenice turned and walked to the door leading to the ship's cabin. "Psychedelic," she muttered as she disappeared through the door. "Of all the words for him to come up with, where did he get that one?"

* * *

After Jenice had left, Michael shook his head and reached inside his wet suit to remove a copy of the captain's map he'd kept there for safe keeping. "We won't be needing this anymore," he said to himself. "It's time we burn it."

Michael knew the copy was no longer needed, so he figured it was safer to destroy it. The original was hidden safely away in a safe-deposit box back home. Opening the boat's supply cabinet, he removed a box of waterproof matches. Striking one, he held it to the edge of the map, which ignited almost instantly. Within seconds it was reduced to ashes, which he dropped overboard.

After taking a few minutes to store away all their gear, Michael started the engine and headed the small craft back in the direction of

Miami, where they had headquartered the past two weeks in preparation for searching out the captain's sunken ship.

* * *

Maggie re-read, for the third time, the celestial memo that had just crossed her desk. She glanced across the office to Gus's desk where he was at work on some project or another. She wasn't sure what. But then, Maggie seldom knew what Gus was working on. Maybe it was better that way. Maggie was a perfectionist who held strictly to the line in working with her clients. She knew all the facts, and knew exactly where her projects stood at all times. Her partner, Gus, on the other hand, would simply dive headlong into his projects, depending on what she saw as blind luck to bring them to a satisfactory conclusion. She had to admit that in the end, he always managed to get the job done—though it was not uncommon for him to experience what she termed "unnecessary difficulties" along the way.

Samantha and Jason's contract was a prime example. Thanks to Gus's typo, the case of Samantha and Jason had turned into a real hassle and one that stretched the patience of the higher authorities nearly to their limits. But, in the end, even the higher authorities were smiling at its conclusion. In their report, they surmised that since Gus had learned much from his mistake, and since Samantha and Jason were happy with the results, the case could be considered closed out with honor.

Still, if Maggie had been a Special Conditions Coordinator at the time, and if she had handled the case . . . Ah, but why even look back now? That was long before she and Gus had been moved upstairs as partners holding the title of Level Two Special Conditions Coordinator. Gus had been a Level One Special Conditions Coordinator back then, and she had been his secretary. Anyway, the case was history now. And, after all, everything came up roses in the end.

Maggie shook away the memory and read the memo again. The purpose of it was clear; the higher authorities wanted Michael and Jenice's case moved to the highest priority. It seemed the higher authorities were aware that some complications were about to show up in the case. The memo was meant for Samantha and Jason, of course. But since Samantha and Jason were off enjoying a two-week vacation in a remote part of the universe, and since Maggie didn't want to bother them with an item of business that would most surely cut their vacation short, she decided to handle the matter herself.

She stood, crossed the room to where Gus was working, and handed him the memo. "You'd better read this," she said. "It's a hot one. I just received it from the higher authorities."

Gus took the memo from her and looked it over. "So what's the big deal, Maggie?" he asked after finishing it. "Ya know perfectly well I've handled hundreds of problems bigger than this back at my old job."

"Yes, Gus. I know about the problems you've handled. The trouble is, I know HOW you handled those problems. We have a touchy situation here, in case you haven't noticed. If Sam get's wind of this, she'll be on the next celestial flight home, in spite of all my efforts. Those two deserve their time away together, Gus."

Gus shrugged. "What the heck. Keepin' Sam in the dark shouldn't be all that big a deal. We just short-circuit the connection' on her celestial e-mail. She won't have a clue."

Maggie threw up both hands. "Won't have a clue? Wake up, Gus. We're talking about Sam's brother here. With Michael in trouble there's no way shutting down Sam's e-mail is going to keep her from finding out about it. I've never seen anything like the powers of detection that woman has. It's uncanny the way she always knows what's going on."

Gus leaned back in his chair and gave the memo a toss to the top of his desk. "Tell ya what, Maggie. How about if Captain Blake and me look after Jenice and Michael? That'll free ya up ta spend all yer energy keepin' Sam in the dark. Is that a deal or what?"

"Oh sure," Maggie sniffed. "Give me the impossible part of the assignment." She thought about it a moment or two. "Maybe you've got a point, Gus. I'm not saying I can keep Sam from finding out what's going on, but I'll stand a lot better chance doing it from here in the office than I would out chasing after Michael and Jenice."

She sighed and gave Gus a long hard look. "You and the captain, eh? Well, okay. But I suggest you get out of that chair and make an appearance where the trouble lies pretty darn fast. From what that memo says, I imagine things will get sticky if they're left unchecked."

* * *

Jenice emerged from the cabin wearing a pair of jeans and a cotton shirt. Since there was a stiff sea breeze blowing, she also wore a light slicker to shield against the ocean spray on the trip back. Michael was at the wheel of the boat. She crept up behind him and encircled him with her arms. "Thanks," she whispered in his ear.

"Thanks?" he laughed. "Thanks for what?"

"Thanks for proving I won't be giving up my dreams by marrying the man of my dreams. This was a wonderful adventure, Michael. And sharing it with you made it all the sweeter."

CHAPTER 5

Stuart Fox slammed his hand against the side of the boat. "This stinks!" he shouted, examining the tracking unit his silent partner had given him. "The boat we're looking for is out there right now, no doubt over the spot where the sunken treasure lies, and this thing the man gave me is of no use whatsoever. It doesn't have a long enough range to pick up the sending device planted on Michael Allen's boat. I'm dealing with an idiot here!" Stuart yelled as he gave a pained look at Max Yorty. "What kind of a man is he? How much trouble would it have been for him to pick up a tracking system with enough range to do the job?"

"Relax, Fox," Max Yorty said, with a pat to Stuart's shoulder. "Me and the boys will find 'em. We got a pretty good fix on the direction they took from our lookout that watched 'em pull out of the harbor this morning."

"Yeah, I'm sure you'll find them, Yorty. But will you find them in time? If we catch them in the water, we know they're directly over the area where the gold lies."

Max shrugged. "You mentioned a map, Fox. All we need is a look-see at that map. I been at this business long enough to find a thumbtack on the bottom of these waters just so I get a look at the map showing where it lies. Ain't no way I'm letting an opportunity like finding a fortune in gold slip away just because I don't have someone to point to the exact spot where it lies hidden."

Stuart knew Max was right. It wasn't the end of the world if they didn't find the boat while the divers were in the water. Still, it would have made this job a lot easier. It really riled him that his silent partner didn't think ahead well enough to foresee this problem. Suddenly, he noticed something. The needle on the tracking device moved. "We got 'em, Yorty," he cried out. "They just moved within range. Shove that throttle open, man. Let's go get ourselves a treasure map!"

* * *

As the boat sped for shore, Michael found it hard to keep his eyes off Jenice. He'd already known that she was the most beautiful woman he had ever seen, but here, in a speeding boat on the high seas, Jenice Anderson seemed to be in her element. Her beauty was only enhanced by nature's touch. He loved the way the afternoon sunlight glistened on her long silky hair, the way her eyes sparkled with the excitement of the moment and her hair flowed in the wind. There was absolutely nothing about Jenice Anderson that Michael didn't love. Reaching for her hand, he pulled her around to face him.

"You don't plan on inviting Roy Jenkins and Bruce Vincent to the wedding, do you?" he asked.

"Yes, Michael, I do intend to invite them; they're my good friends. Why? You're not still jealous because I considered marrying them at one time, are you?"

Michael considered the thought. "Not Bruce," he truthfully admitted. "Bruce is happily married to Arline now. Roy? I don't know. I might be a little jealous of Roy. After all, you were wearing his ring on that rainy day Sam got us together in front of the museum."

Jenice's eyes revealed her shock. True, when Samantha had taken her to the museum where Michael was waiting, Jenice had still been wearing Roy's ring. She had forgotten all about it. But at the time, she thought she had successfully removed it without Michael seeing.

"What do you mean I was wearing Roy's ring?" she stammered. "It was your ring I had on my finger. You're the one who put it there, if you'll remember."

"Oh yeah," Michael laughed. "Like I didn't notice the way you nearly broke your finger trying to remove Roy's ring without me noticing."

Jenice glared at him. "You knew about the ring?" she asked in disbelief. "And you didn't say anything?"

Michael's grin deepened. "I thought I'd save it for sometime when I needed an ace in the hole," he jokingly explained. "You know, to make you squirm a little. Like you're doing now."

Her hands flew to her hips. "Michael Allen! You are incorrigible!"

"Sure, I'm incorrigible," he laughed. "You knew that before you fell in love with me. May I remind you of your own words? *'If you wanted a stay-at-home, sanity-loving sort of wife, you'd have written me off years ago.'* Well, I guess if you wanted a 'corrigible' sort of husband, you'd have written *me* off years ago."

They burst out laughing. "No doubt about it, Miss Anderson," Michael continued. "The two of us were meant for each other. I'd say we're destined for one crazy, incorrigible forever together, wouldn't you?"

"I'd say so, Mr. Allen," she agreed. "Just so long as you never again ask me to spell psychedelic."

Just then, Michael noticed a movement in the distance. He watched as the object grew closer at a rapid speed. It was a boat. One bigger and faster than his and Jenice's. And it appeared to be headed straight for them. "Would you look at this?" he said. "I think we're about to have company."

* * *

Gus glanced up to see who had just burst into his office. It was Captain Blake. Gus had sent the captain out earlier to keep an eye on Michael and Jenice, and now he appeared to be greatly agitated about something.

"What's the problem, pal? Ya look as if ya just saw a ghost." Gus grinned. "Little pun there, pal."

"Aye, matey, and it is a ghost I'll be seein' unless ye comes to the rescue of me friend Michael Allen. He be fixin' to take a keel haulin', says I."

Gus looked confused. "Keel haulin?'" he quizzed. "What are ya talkin' about, Blake?"

"Michael and the lady, Jenice, be findin' themselves the victim of some blackguards of the worst kind, thinks I. They be needin' the kind of help that a second-level angel, like yerself, can be givin', matey. Otherwise, yer observation about me seein' a ghost might just come into port."

Gus stretched out both hands. "Now hold on here, pal. What's all this talk about Michael bein' in trouble? I got work ta do here in the office; I can't be rushin' off for no reason, Blake. If ya want my help, yer gonna hafta tell me exactly what sort of trouble yer talkin' about."

Captain Blake stepped up to look Gus right in the eye. "I be tellin' ye what sort o' trouble YE be in, matey, if YE be not comin' with me to Michael's rescue. YE'LL be on the plank at the tip of a blade held by an angry angel named Sam, says I. It be me suggestion that ye be takin' me word for the problem, and be comin' along with me now. Ye has me word ye'll be sorry if ye does otherwise."

Thoughts of facing an irate Sam were enough to convince Gus. "Ya got a point there, pal," he said grabbing his ball cap and jamming it on his head. "Let's be on our way."

* * *

Jenice watched with keen interest as the approaching craft closed in with the obvious intention of intercepting them. "Who do you think they are, Michael?" she asked nervously.

Michael never took his eyes off the boat. "I'm not sure, but from their looks I'd say they're up to no good."

Jenice studied the situation carefully. It was a large boat, powered by twin outboard engines. It had an enclosed cabin although no insignia was apparent to indicate it was anything other than a privately owned boat. Two men could be seen on the forward deck. Both men were armed. One held a short-barreled shotgun and the other had a pistol tucked inside the belt of his trousers. Michael was right; this didn't look good at all. It definitely left her with a case of the jitters.

"What do you think?" she asked. "Should we make a run for it?"

He gave a half-hearted chuckle. "Not in this boat," he grimaced. "Those guys could run circles around us. I hear these waters are notorious for drug runners, but I can't figure what they might want with us."

A cold shiver passed through Jenice as a staggering thought crossed her mind. What if these men had somehow learned of their reason for being here? What if they knew about the gold? But how could they? Neither she nor Michael had mentioned a word of this to anyone.

"You there!" the man holding the shotgun shouted as the boat moved closer. "Pull up. We wanna talk."

Michael had little choice but to cut the throttle. Within seconds, the intruders were alongside. One of the men secured the two boats together with a rope. Jenice could only hold her breath and look on helplessly as the two stepped aboard their boat. It was then she got her first close look at them. The one holding the shotgun was the largest of the two. He had long black, unruly hair tied in a ponytail at the back of his head, and he looked as if he hadn't shaved in days. On his right bicep was a large tattoo of an octopus with its tentacles wrapped around an ancient-looking sailing vessel. He was grinning menacingly, revealing a large gap between his two upper front teeth. She guessed his age to be somewhere around thirty.

The second man looked a little younger. He, too, wore his hair long, though his hung straight down. He wore a full, unkempt beard and a large gold earring in his right ear. He also had a tattoo on his left forearm. His depicted a snake coiled and ready to strike. If these men weren't drug runners, Jenice concluded, they at least looked the part.

"What do you want from us?" Michael asked, staring down the barrel of the shotgun.

"Did you hear that, Lefty?" the larger man mocked. "He's asking what it is we want. Why do you suppose he would do that?"

"Don't rightly know, Max," Lefty responded. "Could have something to do with the way you're tickling his tonsils with the barrel of that shotgun."

Both men let out a burst of harsh laughter, and Max said, "Rumor has it the two of you are in a possession of a certain map. I want that map and how I get it makes little difference to me."

Jenice shot a glance at Michael. She didn't know he had burnt the only copy of the map they had with them. She supposed it was still tucked in his wet suit, where she had last seen him stash it.

Max's expression hardened as he continued. "We can do this the easy way, or we can do it the hard way. If we do it the easy way, the two of you can be about your business. On the other hand, if you choose the hard way you might find yourselves facing a few problems I'm sure you'd rather not face." He paused to shrug. "Either way I get the map. So what'll it be. The easy way, or . . . ?"

Jenice was still looking at Michael, who now turned to look at her. Their eyes met, and a wave of understanding passed between them. Somehow these men knew about the map and about the gold. "I'm sorry, gentlemen," Michael answered coolly. "I know nothing about any map. But if you need directions someplace . . ."

The big man sneered. "Oh, a smart guy. We got ourselves a smart guy here, Lefty. What do you think we ought to do about that?"

Lefty thought a moment. "I guess we could say, please, Max. That might work."

"Nah! I never was much for all that polite talk." At that moment, Max noticed the leather pouch lying on the control panel. "Well, now, what do we have here?" he asked picking up the pouch and feeling its contents carefully. "Cover 'em, Lefty, while I have a look-see at what's in this little sack." Max propped the shotgun against the side of the boat, and let a few of the coins spill out into his hand. "Would you look at this? I do believe these here people have found themselves some gold coins down there at the bottom of this big ocean."

"We found nothing in the ocean," Jenice interrupted. "Those coins were a gift from my uncle."

Max eyed her skeptically. "You expect me to believe a story like that, missy? What would your uncle be doing with coins like these?"

"He's a collector," she spit back. "And don't go getting too attached to them, buster. Just remember, who they belong to."

Max moved closer to Jenice. "You're a spunky one, aren't you? I like my women spunky." He reached out a hand as if to touch her face. She slapped it aside. "We'll just let that go for now," he said, glaring at her. He returned the sampling of coins to the pouch and closed it. "These coins are still wet," he noted. "I say they came off the ocean floor. And I say there's a map showing exactly where they came from. I want that map. Where is it, lady?"

"I have no idea what you're talking about," Jenice stalled in an icy voice. "The coins were a gift from my uncle. End of story."

Squinting his eyes and peering at her, Max raised the shotgun under Jenice's chin. "You listen to me. I know you have the map, and I want it. Now cough it up."

"Leave her alone!" Michael snapped. "You got something to say, say it to me. Man to man. That is if you really are a man? Without that gun, I'd have my doubts."

Fire blazed from Max's eyes as his attention shifted to Michael. "You got a big mouth, mister. Now unless you wanna be shark food, I suggest you cut the stall. Where's the map?"

Jenice quickly surveyed the situation. Max's shotgun was still pointing in her direction, but Max was now looking at Michael. Lefty had yanked the pouch of coins from Max's hand and was examining its contents for himself. She made a split-second decision. Grabbing the shotgun by the barrel, she forced it away from the unsuspecting man. Before he could recover, she gave him a spinning karate kick to the side of his head. Max hit the deck of the boat with a tremendous thud.

It took Michael less than a second to realize what Jenice was up to. He quickly joined in, taking Lefty out with a body slam while simultaneously disarming him.

By the time the two men regained their senses, Michael had them covered with Lefty's pistol. "What do you know about that?!" Michael exclaimed. "I was right, Max. You aren't much of a man without that gun, are you?"

Max rubbed his throbbing face. "She got me with a karate kick," he moaned. "The broad knows karate."

Jenice stared at Max. She reached down and picked up Michael's scuba mask still lying where he had thrown it earlier. Holding the mask by its strap, she dipped it in the ocean and retrieved it filled with cold water. This she dumped over Max's head. "That's for calling me a broad," she said. "Count yourself lucky, sport. The last jerk who called me that ended up in traction."

At that precise moment, a deafening explosion split the stillness of the late morning air. Jenice instantly recognized it as a gunshot. She turned to see where the shot had come from. To her horror, she saw there was a third man aboard the intruder's boat. He had previously remained out of sight below deck. This man seemed out of place in company with the others. He appeared neat and well groomed, and wore a business suit. He was also holding a pistol.

In the chaos of the moment, Jenice had forgotten about Michael until she heard his moan. Spinning to look, her heart shot to her throat as she realized Michael had been hit by the gunfire.

"Michael!" she screamed and rushed to his side, cradling his head in her arms. His eyes were closed, and he didn't appear to be breathing. She felt something warm on her hand. She pulled it up and found it covered with Michael's blood. "WHAT HAVE YOU DONE?" she screamed. "YOU'VE KILLED HIM!"

* * *

Michael heard the sound of the explosion, but he couldn't figure out where it had come from. Then came the throbbing in his head, a terrible throbbing. Looking down at his own hand, he could see still holding the pistol taken from Lefty. His hand didn't seem to be wounded, but there was blood on it. The blood appeared to be trickling onto his hand from somewhere higher up. Someone must have been shot, he reasoned hazily, not realizing the blood was his own. His eyes grew blurry as he watched the fingers of his hand relax, allowing the pistol to fall to the deck of the boat. Suddenly, his legs would no longer hold him. Slowly, he sank to the floor of the boat.

Darkness was closing in. Someone called his name. He tried to answer, but no sound would form in his throat. *Jenice,* he thought. *Where is she? I can't find her.* Everything was black now. Black and quiet. And then, the sweet kiss of unconsciousness eased the throbbing pain into a blissful nothingness.

* * *

"Bring the lady," the man in the business suit instructed calmly. "We'll plant some stuff on the body and leave him in the boat. That way when they find him they'll figure he was taken out in a drug deal gone bad."

"Why not just toss the body overboard, boss?"

"No, you fool! They're going to find the boat anyway. They might as well find a body with it. That way they'll figure he was a druggie, and that will be the end of it."

Jenice hadn't even noticed that Max had his gun back until she felt the cold barrel against the side of her temple. "Maybe next time you'll think twice before kicking me in the head," he growled. "Now get up, broad. We're going for a little boat ride."

"No!" she gasped. "You can't just leave him here like this! He needs help!"

Max grabbed Jenice's arm and pulled her up. "Forget him, lady. He's beyond help now. And that's what's going to happen to you if you don't produce the map we're looking for."

Struggling was of little use with three guns pointed her way. Max jerked her away from Michael and forced her onto the waiting boat. Once there, her hands were cuffed behind her back.

Jenice's heart sank as she watched the men strip Michael of all his identification and plant what appeared to be a pouch of white powder on him. She guessed it was illegal drugs of some sort. She strained to see the slightest sign of movement from Michael, but he lay perfectly still. The men took great pains to search him and she knew they would find the map. But they didn't and she could only wonder if he had destroyed it without her knowing. Had he hidden it someplace on the boat? She just didn't know, but she was greatly relieved these men didn't find it.

After the men led her back to the larger boat, Jenice was forced to lie face-down on the deck as it sped away. Never had she felt so helpless. She was no stranger to crime scenes, since covering crimes was a major part of her job as a reporter—but this time was different. This time the victim wasn't just some stranger's face in the night. This time it was Michael. And there was nothing she could do to help him. All she could do was lie there, on the bottom of a boat bound for who knew where.

CHAPTER 6

Samantha stared at the gorgeous green dress displayed in the window of Casual Universe, one of the finest shopping places she had yet seen on this side of forever. Maggie was right—this celestial mall was every celestial shopper's dream come true. And if ever there was a woman who loved shopping, it was Samantha Hackett. Why then couldn't she relax and enjoy this time alone with her crazy little ghost, Jason? Why did these feelings of concern keep popping up in her mind? Again, she looked longingly at the dress. Green had always been her favorite color, and this dress just seemed to have her name written all over it. Disgusted with her lack of excitement, she turned to face Jason. She didn't say a word. She didn't have to.

"Okay, my cute little angel wife," he said, admiring her through narrowed eyes. "What is your problem? This is a great anniversary gift the gang showered on us, so why aren't you enjoying it?"

"I don't know what's the matter, Jason," she replied. "You know me and my intuition. I can't help it if something doesn't feel right."

Jason threw up his hands. "What's not to feel right? Personally, I can't find one thing wrong exploring this far-out universe. And I haven't even had the chance to check out any of the fantastic restaurants here yet."

"I know all that, Jason. But I can't help how I feel. Do you have your celestial cell phone with you?"

"Sam? You're not thinking of calling Maggie . . . ?"

"What can it hurt, Jason? Maybe if I hear her tell me everything is okay . . ."

"All right, Sam," Jason said, digging the phone out of his pocket. "Do what you think you have to, but I think it's foolish." Shoving both hands in his pockets, Jason watched as she called up Maggie's office number.

* * *

A myriad of thoughts passed through Jenice's mind as she lay on the floor of the speeding boat that took her farther and farther away from Michael. Was he alive? If so, would he receive help in time? And the biggest question of all, would she ever see him again?

She closed her eyes in a frantic effort to control the pain. The physical pain, brought on by being handcuffed and thrown face-down on the bottom of the boat was only a fraction of the pain tearing at her heart. How had this happened? How had these people learned about the captain's gold? Where were they taking her? And her beloved Michael . . . could he really be dead? How would she go on without him? These questions haunted her with maddening persistence as she listened to the roar of the powerful twin engines taking the craft farther and farther away from the man she loved.

After a period of time, which she estimated to be about half an hour, the engines were throttled back. Seconds later, she felt a jar as the boat bumped another object. At first, she supposed it was a docking pier. Wherever it was, there were voices. More voices than just those of Max, Lefty, and the third man in the business suit. Maybe four—maybe six more voices, it was hard to tell. They were male voices and were concentrating on a single subject—the question about the map showing the location of the sunken gold.

Suddenly, Jenice was pulled to her feet. She found herself looking directly into the evil eyes of the one called Max. It was then she realized they weren't at a pier at all. They were still afloat somewhere in the ocean. The jar she felt was a result of the boat coming in contact with a much larger craft. A very large yacht.

"Move it, little lady," Max snapped, shoving her roughly toward a rope ladder ascending to the deck of the yacht.

Jenice stared at the ladder. "You expect me to climb this with my hands cuffed behind my back?" she asked, trying to keep her voice emotionless. No sense letting these low-life ruffians know they were getting to her.

Max grumbled and dug through his pocket until he found the key. Then he removed the cuffs. Jenice rubbed her wrists where the metal had dug painfully into her flesh. As she did, she noticed blood on the slicker she had put on when she changed out of the wetsuit earlier. Michael's blood. She closed her eyes, feeling faint.

"Up the ladder, missy," Max instructed. "You got two hands now."

Jenice ignored him and removed the slicker, which she tossed to the deck of the boat. She didn't need this reminder of Michael's condition. If she was going to escape, she couldn't afford to let her mind become consumed with the fear that he might not be alive, that she might never see him again.

"Up the ladder, I said. Now quit stalling," Max grumbled again. "We ain't got all day."

Jenice grabbed the ladder and placed one foot on the first rung. As she did, she looked around. All she could see in every direction was ocean. A glance upward revealed the hardened faces of a half dozen men staring at her over the ship's railing. With Max right behind her, she forced herself to ascend the ladder.

"How about it, little lady?" Max asked, as he stepped onto the deck of the yacht. "Are you ready to cooperate now?"

Jenice glared at the man. Then, catching him completely off guard, she lifted her foot and raked it hard down the front of his shin. Grimacing in pain, Max leaned down and grabbed his leg as if that would stop the throbbing. Seconds later he stood and would have backhanded her forcefully if not for the man in the business suit, who prevented it by grabbing Max's hand.

"All in good time, my friend," he cautioned. "We wouldn't want to do anything that might cause her to forget where the map is. I promise, Max, if she fails to cooperate, I'll let you mess her up all you like." He turned to Jenice and placing a hand on her chin, gently raised her head until their eyes met. "Of course, if you do cooperate, I see no need for you to be hurt."

Snapping her head to one side, Jenice managed to sink her teeth into the man's thumb hard enough to bring a sprinkling of blood.

With a sharp moan, he withdrew his hand. For several seconds he glared at her with vengeance in his expression. Then he relaxed and let his face form into a smile. "You are a spirited one, aren't you?" he said.

Jenice laughed bravely. "And you, sir, are despicable. Tell me, do you have a name, or do they just whistle when they want you to come looking for a bone?"

He stiffened noticeably but managed to keep his smile in place. "I have a name. Stuart Fox. This is Max Yorty, and over here we have Lefty Nelson." He pointed to each in turn as he gave their names. "We'll be your hosts for the next little while. Just how long that will be depends on you, my dear." He paused, allowing his smile to deepen although it never reached his eyes. "There's no reason we can't all come out winners in this little venture, Miss Anderson. Rumor has it the load of gold we're talking about here is a pretty big one. They say it will bring a sizable fortune. The way I see it, there should be enough to go around for everyone involved. Think about it. You can come out of this a wealthy woman, simply by sharing the wealth with the rest of us. And your end of the bargain will be risk-free. My organization will take care of the dirty work, pulling the stuff off the bottom of the Atlantic, that sort of thing. That's what I'd call a real deal."

"Ha!" she laughed. "It's more what I'd call the raving of a madman. Like I told your goons, I don't know anything about this hidden gold you're talking about. I had twelve coins that my uncle gave me. Nothing more, nothing less."

Stuart turned a deaf ear to her obvious contempt, but a look of curiosity crossed his face. "This man you were with, Michael Allen, what was he to you, anyway? Was he just a partner, or was there more to your relationship than that?"

His question caught Jenice by complete surprise. What possible motive could this man have for asking such a thing? "Whatever might be between Michael and me is none of your concern," she said icily.

"No, of course it's not," Stuart replied. "But I do have a reason for asking. And rather than tell you my reason, why don't I just show you?"

His words confused Jenice more than ever. "Am I supposed to have the slightest idea what you're talking about?" she asked stiffly. "Because I don't."

"I'm talking about an old friend of yours, Miss Anderson. Someone I know you were once serious about, and I suspect you may still have a soft place in your heart for him. He just happens to be right here, on this yacht. Please step this way, and I'll take you to him."

Jenice was dumbfounded. An old friend? Who could it possibly be? She couldn't even venture a guess. Stuart pointed the way to a staircase leading up to a higher level of the ship. Realizing there would be little use in resisting, Jenice stepped out and ascended the stairs with Stuart just behind her. "To your left," he said as they reached the top of the stairs. "The door marked with the number six."

Jenice stopped in front of the door. Stuart inserted a key in the dead bolt lock and gave it a twist. He pushed it open and motioned for her to step inside. She glanced at the dead bolt, then at Stuart. "You want me inside so you can keep me prisoner under lock and key. Is that your plan?"

"I want you to step inside so you can meet the man who's our guest in this cabin. Your cabin is just down the hall. I'll take you there later."

Jenice drew a quick breath and stepped through the door into the cabin. Stuart remained in the hallway. "I'll leave you two alone to enjoy your reunion," he said. "I'll be back later, of course, to escort you to your own cabin." With this, he closed and locked the door.

Even before there was time to turn around, she heard someone calling her name. "Jenice?! Good heavens, it is you!"

"Roy?" she gasped in astonishment, turning to face him. "Roy Jenkins? I don't understand. What are you doing here?"

Roy stepped forward and placed his hand on the side of Jenice's face. "The question is," he asked, gazing at her with grave concern. "What are YOU doing here?"

"What am I doing here? I've been abducted, Roy, that's what I'm doing here."

Roy backed up a step and looked at her. "But I don't understand. I thought you were still out on the West Coast. How did you manage to get mixed up with this bunch of thugs?"

Jenice's mind raced. There was no longer any doubt what these men wanted with her, but Roy Jenkins? What could they possibly want with Roy? Then it hit her. From what Stuart had said, it was obvious he believed there was a strong link between Jenice and Roy. Stuart must have gotten word that she and Roy were once engaged. She cringed at the thought of what all this could mean. It could be Stuart's intention to threaten Roy's life in an effort to get information out of her. Stuart was obviously a dangerous man who would stop at nothing to get what he wanted. Jenice shuddered at the thought and wondered how she might handle the problem should it actually occur.

"I have been on the West Coast, Roy," she explained. "Michael and I—that is we . . ." She stopped in mid sentence just to stare at Roy, and after a moment, asked, "You do know Michael and I are . . ." There was a sudden catch in her voice as she thought, *If Michael is still alive, that is.* Then she forced herself to continue, ". . . planning to be married, don't you?"

A questioning look crossed Roy's face. "You're planning to marry someone? This is a surprise." His hands clenched into fists and he turned away. "Sorry, Jenice," he said. "I guess I'm not over the fact you turned me down just yet. And hearing there's someone else now . . ." He forced a smile and faced her again. "Forgive me, Jenice. It was just a bit of a shock."

Suddenly Roy noticed Jenice's right hand, which was still covered with Michael's dried blood. "What's this?" he asked, reaching for her hand to get a closer look. "Have you been hurt?"

Jenice looked at her own hand. "No," she said, trying to blot the picture of Michael, lying alone and wounded, from her mind. "It's not my blood. There was a shooting—when they abducted me." She exhaled loudly. "Is there somewhere I can wash up?"

His face was horrified. "Those low-life—" He caught himself. "Over there," he said pointing to a bathroom door. "There's a sink inside. Help yourself."

She nodded and stepped inside the bathroom. A feeling of sharp nausea gripped her as she watched Michael's blood being washed down the drain. For nearly a minute she stood there, fighting back the pain. At last, she picked up a clean towel from the counter and dried her hands, then returned to the main cabin where Roy was waiting.

"You mentioned a gunshot," Roy said. "Who was hurt? Was it your friend? Michael?"

"Yes," she said, lowering her eyes as she spoke. "It was Michael."

"Those scum!" Roy spun and slammed the heel of his hand against the wall of his cabin. Taking a deep breath, he let his eyes meet hers. "I'm so sorry, Jenice. How bad was Michael hurt?"

"I'm not sure, Roy." Jenice's voice trailed off as for the first time a flood of deep emotion washed over her. She swallowed. "His head was bleeding badly," she explained. "I couldn't tell for sure if he was breathing. They dragged me away so fast . . ."

Roy stepped forward. Sliding an arm around Jenice, he pulled her head to his chest. "They'll find him," he comforted. "These Florida waters are widely traveled. Someone will find him soon. I'm sure of it."

Jenice closed her eyes tightly. "I can only hope so, Roy." For several minutes she stood with her face buried in Roy's chest. He did nothing to disturb her until she was ready to move away from him. She cleared her throat. "Michael and I met a long time ago, Roy. We just recently got back together, and . . ."

Roy released a loud breath and moved a hand to the back of his neck. "And the chemistry was there, right?" he asked.

She nodded. "Yes, Roy. The chemistry was there. I'm sorry for the way I let you down, but—"

A faint smile returned to his lips. "Hey, say no more, kid. I knew from square one the real chemistry wasn't there with us." He shrugged. "Not on your end, anyway. So tell me, girl, who is this Michael fellow? Someone worthy of you, I hope."

Jenice's eyes fell at the mention of Michael's name. Again, the pains stabbed at her heart. Her mind pictured Michael lying still as death in the boat as she had last seen him. Was he worthy of her? Oh yes, he was worthy of her, all right. The question is, was she worthy of him? Memories of how she had once left him standing in the Paris rain tore at her with a vengeance. He had asked her to marry him at the end of that wonderful summer in Paris. She didn't even have the decency to face him. She had just left him standing there. Now, in light of the fact she might never see him again, the horror of what she had done came with even greater force to her troubled mind.

"Yes," she said emphatically. "Michael is a guy worth all my love. You remember the day on the Caribbean island when you helped airlift me out to get medical help? He was there, too."

Roy's eyes glazed over as he searched his memory of the day Jenice referred to. "The one who was there with Brad Douglas?" he asked.

Jenice swallowed, and nodded yes.

"I see," Roy said soberly. "Then Michael is the artist you told me about when you accepted my ring. You never mentioned his name, you know—which brings up a question. Why did you accept my ring if you and Michael were that close to getting together?"

"It's a long story, Roy. Would you mind terribly if we let it go for now? And while you're at it, would you mind explaining to me why you're on this yacht with these goons?"

Jenice could tell that Roy really didn't want to drop the subject of Michael, but he was courteous enough to honor her feelings. "These men," Roy explained, "are the nucleus of a wide-spread drug empire. I've been working on the story for a couple of months now. It seems that somehow these guys found me out. They broke into my apartment one day last week. And, to put it in their words, I've been a guest on this yacht ever since. This morning they were joined by a new face. I watched him come aboard through the porthole over there. I also watched them bring you aboard, Jenice."

"I see," she responded quietly.

"The man I first saw this morning is the same man who brought you here to my room. Stuart Fox, I heard him called." Roy paused, then added, "I have no idea what these goons have in mind, but to their credit they have kept me fairly comfortable."

Jenice shook her head. "You call being held captive comfortable? Frankly I can think of other words to describe it. There has to be a way to escape. Somehow I have to get back to Michael."

"I'm sure there is, Jenice. They're thorough, but they will make a mistake sooner or later. And when they do, I plan on making my move." Roy's voice was determined, and with a grim chuckle, he asked, "So how did you manage to get your name on the guest list?"

Jenice rubbed her wrists where the cuffs had been. "Michael and I were out in our small boat. Stuart Fox and two of his goons jumped us. That's when they shot Michael."

"Michael's going to be fine, Jenice," Roy comforted her again. "Your first concern right now has to be finding a way out of our own situation. We've got to find a way to escape before these men decide they have no further use for us."

Jenice did her best to push aside the flow of emotion that had overtaken her so violently. She considered just how much she should tell Roy. They had been friends and co-workers for more than five years. If Roy couldn't be trusted, then who could? She came to the conclusion to go for broke.

"There's something you should know, Roy," she began. "These men may not want us dead at all. Not just yet, anyway." She swallowed, and took in a quick breath. "You see, Michael and I weren't just out joyriding when they found us. We had something much more serious going than mere recreation. Something our friends here somehow got wind of."

Roy's next remark came as a real jolt to Jenice. "Would this by any chance have something to do with a certain treasure map?"

"You know about the map?" she gasped. "How?"

"I've heard talk all morning about a treasure map. These walls aren't thick enough to keep everything out."

"It's true, Roy," Jenice exclaimed. "Michael and I do have a map. That's what we were doing off the coast right now."

"What are you saying, Jenice? Is there really a treasure lying out there somewhere for the taking?"

"It's true, Roy. Michael and I found it."

"And these men? They know about the map?"

Jenice nodded. "They know. I haven't admitted anything yet, but they know."

"Where is the map now?" Roy asked. "Someplace safe, I hope. I'm not sure about me, but I'd guess the map is what's keeping you alive."

"The map is in a safe place, and it's going to stay there." She let the subject go at that and asked, "You mentioned escape? Do you have a plan?"

He shrugged. "Not really. I've just been looking for an opening. I figure one will come, and when it does—I'm out of here. Or should I say *we're* out of here?"

"You better believe it's we. And when we do get out, what do you say the two of us join forces to put these guys away where they belong?"

Roy laughed. "Just like old times, eh? I'm sure there's room for one more notch on the belt."

Suddenly, they were interrupted by the sound of the cabin door opening. Jenice turned to see Stuart Fox enter the room. "Talking escape plans, are we?" Stuart smiled. "It makes a good subject, I suppose. But I wouldn't recommend you go any further than discussing the subject. It could become very hazardous to your health."

"You monster!" Jenice cried out. "You had this cabin bugged!"

"Please, Miss Anderson, don't think of me as a monster. I'm really quite a nice individual at heart. A little greedy, maybe. But—"

Jenice glared at him. "How do you know my name?" she demanded.

"Let's just say I've done my research," he laughed. "You see, Miss Anderson, I pride myself on being an opportunist. And at the moment, I see opportunity in the shape of a fortune in gold. Now that I've heard you admit the map really does exist, that opportunity looks even brighter. Is my meaning coming through loud enough?"

"Loud and clear, Mr. Fox," Jenice spit back. "But the chances of your ever seeing this illusionary opportunity materialize into something tangible are what you might call slim to none. Sorry to slam the door on your little dream, but that's life in the big city."

Stuart forced a laugh. "You talk brave for now, Miss Anderson. Let's see if you don't change your mind after being a guest aboard my yacht the next few days. Or—longer if necessary. Please, Miss Anderson, if you'll be so kind as to come with me now, I'll show you to your cabin."

* * *

Maggie hung up the phone and for several seconds sat tapping her fingers against her desktop. She was snapped from her thoughts as Gus entered the office. "Gus," she called to him. "Am I glad to see you. Sam just contacted me, and as I feared, she's having second thoughts about being out of the office right now. I don't know what it is with that lady, but she has a gift for knowing when something isn't going exactly right. I told her everything is fine on this end." Maggie paused with a stern look in Gus's direction. "Everything is fine, isn't it?" she asked. "You and Captain Blake do have the situation with Michael and Jenice in hand, right?"

Gus shrugged. "We sorta ran into a bit of a problem. Nothin' big, ya understand."

"A problem?" Maggie shot back. "What sort of problem?"

Gus rubbed his forehead nervously. "Nothin' big, Maggie," he stated uneasily. "Michael just sorta—well, he went and got hisself . . ."

"Got himself what?" Maggie pressed as Gus hesitated.

Gus shrugged again. "Sorta got hisself shot, is all."

"WHAT!" Maggie shouted. "GOT HIMSELF SHOT?! Gus! I depended on you to hold up your end of this project. How is he, for heaven sakes? You didn't let him get killed, did you?"

Gus walked to his desk where he flopped down in his chair. Picking up a pencil, he played with it worriedly. "Ya got nothin' ta be upset about, Maggie. It's not like the ceilin' would come tumblin' down if Michael did go and get hisself killed," he argued. "Jason and Samantha were on opposite sides of the line, and ya got to admit, things worked out just fine for them."

"Gus Winkelbury! I just this minute gave Sam my word that things were going well on this end, and now you come in here and tell me you've allowed Michael to get himself killed? How am I supposed to face her now? Will you kindly answer that for me, Gus?"

* * *

There was one small porthole in Jenice's cabin and she checked it out. It was too small for a possible escape route, but at least it did provide a view of the outside. That was something, though for the present all she could see was a section of empty deck below her cabin and a long stretch of open ocean.

She checked her door. Just as she supposed, it was locked tight. Next, she checked the room for possible bugging devices. She found two, one fastened to the inside of a lampshade and the second taped to the under side of a nightstand next to the bed. She drew a glass of water from the sink and dropped both devices into it, instantly shorting them out and making them useless. This done, she fell to the bed and lay gazing at the ceiling.

Not surprisingly her thoughts turned once again to Michael. Feeling the tears come to her eyes, she forced them back. Michael had to still be alive. She refused to believe otherwise. As Roy had said, someone was bound to have found him. Possibly by chance—or possibly by design. After all, Michael had a very protective sister who just happened to be an angel.

After a while, her mind drifted to another matter. It was obvious that Stuart Fox had first supposed that she and Roy were more than just friends. She was sure this misconception had been cleared up in his mind after hearing the bugged conversation from Roy's cabin. But this still didn't erase the fact that she and Roy had been the best of friends, and she was certain Stuart realized this. There was no denying it—with Stuart willing to use any means to achieve his design, Roy's life was definitely in danger.

Well, she told herself firmly, *no use worrying about that before it becomes a problem. We'll cross that bridge when we come to it.*

CHAPTER 7

The first thing Michael noticed as he opened his eyes was the brightness of the light he found himself staring directly into. Where was he? What had happened? All he could remember was a deafening explosion followed by a gigantic headache. He tried to force his mind into answers about where he was now, but the brightness of the light was all-consuming. It seemed to engulf him, and he could think of nothing else. Then it hit him. "I'm dead," he gasped. "The stories of being greeted by a brilliant light are all true."

Almost without thinking, he gave himself a quick pat down. "I still feel like myself, if that means anything."

"No, matey, that be no way to tell if ye be alive or if ye be dead," came a voice from somewhere behind him. "Bein' dead feels no different to one's self than bein' alive, says I."

"I know that voice," Michael said. "I've heard it before. Who are you, friend?"

"I be Captain Horatio Symington Blake," came the immediate response.

Michael pressed his hand to his head. Oh, how it ached. That blasted bright light in his eyes didn't help one bit either. "Captain Horatio Symington Blake?" he repeated. "Well, tell me, Captain Blake, do you know where I am at the moment?"

"Aye, matey, I be knowin' where ye are. And I be here to sign ye on to a tour that will take ye far away from this place. There be work to do, says I."

Try as he would, Michael couldn't get his brain focused clear enough to make heads or tails out of what was happening. "What tour? What work?" he asked feebly. "And why is that light in my eyes? Am I dead? Are you an angel here to pick me up—is that what you mean by taking me far away from this place?"

Captain Blake stepped in closer so Michael could get a better look at his face. The man sported a full black beard, but Michael could see his smile clearly through it. In the midst of this hallucination, a humorous thought came to mind. If he was dead, and if this was an angel sent here to take him home, why was he dressed in a pirate's costume?

* * *

"Gus Winkelbury!" Maggie scolded loudly. "Will you tell me just how I'm supposed to face Samantha when she gets back? I positively assured her that all was well on this end, and now you come in here and tell me you've allowed Michael to be killed?"

"Ya weren't listenin' to me, Maggie," Gus explained. "I said Michael got hisself shot; I didn't say he got hisself killed. I was just makin' an observation that even if he had been killed, we could still work things out. Fortunately, I got to him in time ta deflect the bullet so it only left him with a headache—and one other little thing."

Maggie stood and placed both hands on her hips. "One other thing?" she mocked. "And that would be?"

Gus snapped the pencil he was holding in half and stared at the broken ends. "He's havin' a problem rememberin' who he is," Gus explained. "Nothin' serious. His memory will come back in a day or so."

Maggie was so relieved at the revelation that Michael was still alive that the news about his memory loss seemed almost anti-climactic. She was sure Gus had planned it that way, hinting at Michael's death the way he had. But that was Gus. "Where's Michael now?" she pressed.

"I made sure he was rescued, Maggie. He's in the hospital in Miami." Gus took a deep breath. "Under police guard," he added, lowering his voice until it was barely audible.

Maggie covered her eyes as a grimace spread over her face. "Dare I ask what you mean by police guard?"

"Hey, it's okay. The captain is there with him even as we speak. And I got a plan all worked out ta get him out of the hospital and onto the job of trackin' down those guys who kidnapped Jenice."

Maggie's legs felt like rubber. "Jenice has been kidnapped?" she asked. "Wonderful, that's just what I needed to hear. All right, Gus. That's it. As of this instant, you can consider me your shadow in this case. I'm not taking my eyes off you again. Do you hear me, Gus?"

* * *

Michael stared up at the man in the pirate's costume. "I'm dead, right?" he asked. "And you're the angel sent here to pick me up?"

Captain Blake smiled and caught Michael off guard with his next comment. "Nay, matey, ye be not dead. Ye came close, says I. But me friend Gus managed to show up just in time to save yer life."

Michael strained to remember. "Save my life from what?" he asked.

"From the powder and ball, matey. Ye be shot in the head. Me friend Gus got there too late to stop the gun from firin', but he did manage to twist the path of the ball so it barely scrapped the side of yer head, says I. Ye be lyin' in a sick bay at the moment. And ye be starin' into the ceiling light. It only seems bright to ye, because your eyes have been closed these many hours."

Michael rolled onto his side where he lay looking at the very blurry figure of a man. He squinted and tried to focus. Little by little, the fellow came into clearer view. He sported a full beard, just as he had earlier, and he was still wearing some sort of pirate's costume. The only thing missing was the parrot on his shoulder.

Now that Michael's vision was working somewhat better, he looked more closely at his surroundings. The pirate was right; he was in a sick bay, so to speak. Actually it was a hospital room. A private room, at that. He noticed the door leading to the nurse's station was closed. The upper half of the door was frosted glass, but it was transparent enough to reveal the shadowy outline of a man just on the other side of it.

Michael's attention returned to the pirate. "I keep thinking I should know you," he remarked. "But I can't bring to mind from where." Captain Blake continued smiling, but made no effort to jog Michael's memory.

A sound at the door caught Michael's attention. He looked to see a man had stepped into the room. The man wore a pair of black trousers, a white shirt and black tie, and of all things—a nearly floor-length tan overcoat! Who did this guy think he was, Columbo?

Michael forced himself up to a sitting position as the man approached his bed. He looked around for any sign of the pirate, but the fellow had vanished.

"Well, slick," the man in the overcoat said to Michael. "We woke up, did we?"

"Yeah," Michael managed to respond. "I'm awake, but boy do I have a headache."

"No question you should have a headache, son. Gunshots to the head have a tendency to cause headaches. My name's Darwell. Detective Curtis Darwell," he said, flashing an official-looking badge. "I'd like to ask you a couple of questions about something we found on your person when the Coast Guard boarded your boat." The detective shoved the badge back in his pocket and pulled out a clear plastic bag which he held up for Michael to see. The bag contained a white powdery-looking substance. "Would you care to comment on this, son?"

Michael was confused. "Boat? Coast Guard? I'm sorry, sir, but I don't know what you're talking about."

The detective threw up both hands, took one step away from the bed, did an about-face, and moved to within inches of Michael's face.

"Now listen, son!" he nearly shouted. "What do you say we don't start with this loss of memory thing. Play it straight with me, okay? Where'd you get this stuff?"

"I'm telling you, I don't know what you're talking about. I don't remember anything about a boat, and I've never seen that package before in my life. You've got to believe me, I'm telling you the truth."

"The truth? Sure you are, son. And next you'll be telling me you can't remember your own name. That is where this is leading, isn't it?"

"My name? Of course I know my name. I'm . . ." Michael tried to brush away the fog from his mind. Why couldn't he say his own name? "Something is wrong. Something bad. I can't remember who I am. Someone help me, please."

"Look, son, I'm not buying it. Either you cooperate with me or I'll make you wish you'd never been born. I don't believe you're the head honcho I'm looking for, but I do believe whoever sold you this stuff is that guy. And I want him. Think about it. I can see to it you walk away from this smelling like a rose. Or I can throw you in the dungeon and feed the key to the dragon. What's it gonna be, son?"

"I'm sorry, Detective—" said a doctor who entered the room and stepped between Darwell and Michael's bed, "—but this man is in no condition to have you questioning him just yet. If you'll kindly step outside . . ."

Darwell slapped an open palm to his forehead. "Come on, Doc! Just give me five minutes with this guy, that's all I need. Then he can get all the rest in the world for all I care."

"Not five minutes, not one second," the doctor firmly stated, taking hold of the detective's arm and nudging him toward the door. "I'll let you know when this man can be questioned. Until then, his room is off limits to you and to your fellow officers."

Darwell pulled a pencil and note pad from his pocket and scribbled something on it. "What is it with all you do-gooder hospital folks, anyway? These are criminals we're dealing with here. How do you expect guys like me to protect people like you from these criminals if you won't let me do my job?" He closed the note pad and shoved it and the pencil back in his pocket.

"You can do your job, Detective. Just as soon as I do mine and get this man well enough to be interrogated. And not one second sooner."

Darwell reached out and straightened the doctor's shirt collar. "Okay, Doc, we'll do it your way. But my man stands guard at the door to this room, ya got that? No one comes in or out without his say-so. And I do mean no one. And I want all the nurses to have your personal okay. Are we on the same wavelength here, pal?"

The doctor drew in a quick breath. "I'll see to it that only qualified hospital staff attend to this man. But if your guard tries to keep my people out, I warn you there will be a statement to the press. And I doubt you want the press involved."

"Ya got that right, Doc. I'm not known for my love of the press. Let's just keep this between ourselves, okay. I won't stand in the way of you doctoring this man, and you don't stand in the way of my keeping him under tight custody. We got a deal, pal?"

"I told you, only professional hospital staff will be allowed in here. That's all the deal you'll get out of me, Detective."

Darwell shook his head and left the room, at which point the doctor returned to Michael's bed. After checking his pulse and listening to his heart, the doctor proceeded to remove the tubes and paraphernalia from him and disconnected the automatic monitor. "I don't think you'll be needing this any longer," he explained. "The staff will keep a close check on your condition. And that I promise, in spite of our friend, the detective."

"Thank you, doctor. It does feel good getting all those needles out of me."

The doctor smiled and left the room, closing the door behind himself. Michael leaned back, resting his aching head on the pillow while straining to think. *What is happening to me? I can't even remember my name. All I remember is the sound of a gunshot, and feeling as if my head had exploded from my shoulders. And what is it this Detective Darwell's getting at? Is he accusing me of drug dealing? That's preposterous. I would never stoop to dealing in drugs.* He paused in deeper thought. *Would I? How can I say I wouldn't deal in drugs when I don't even know who I am?*

* * *

Samantha stared at the name tag on the celestial travel agent who just stood there wearing a foolish grin. "Well, Miss Cassandra Jean," she said, without the slightest attempt at hiding the sarcasm in her voice. "Let me see if I've got this straight. You're telling me there's no way Jason and I can return to our own galaxy until the two-week scheduled tour is up?"

"I'm sorry, Mrs. Hackett. But what can I do?" Cassandra excused meekly. "The lady who booked your celestial tour put a stipulation on the package. She was adamant about you finishing your vacation. I wish there was something I could do, but it's all here in the fine print." Cassandra held up the contract for Samantha to see, her finger on the paragraph stipulating that no transportation would be provided for an early return home.

Samantha turned to Jason. "Maggie did this to me? Why, Jason? Why would she do such a thing?"

"It's obvious," Jason shrugged. "Maggie wanted you to enjoy the whole two weeks, and she knows you well enough to realize you might pull this very thing."

Samantha put both hands on her hips. "I don't care what it takes. I want to go home *now!*"

Cassandra looked unhappy. "I hope you understand, ma'am. My hands are tied in the matter. I only work here; I don't make the rules."

Jason took Samantha by the arm. "Come on, let's go. We're wasting our time in this place."

"I will not leave!" Samantha huffed, pulling her arm free from Jason's hold. "My intuition tells me I'm needed at home, and my intuition tells me it's because Michael is in trouble. You know my intuition is never wrong, Jason. You've got to reason with this woman. I mean it, you do whatever it takes to get us a ride home."

Jason looked stunned. "You think Michael is in trouble?" he asked.

"Yes I do, Jason. And don't ask me how I know, I just know."

Jason thought a moment. "All right," he said at length. "If you're that certain we have to get home, I think I know a way. Come on, let's go."

Samantha was hesitant. "What are you talking about, Jason? This is the department we have to deal with to get transportation home."

"No, Sam, it's not. These folks have their orders. Trust me, I know another way. I'll get you home, lady. Come on. What do you say we go pay a visit to a friend of mine?"

* * *

After the doctor left his room, Michael drifted off to sleep. He wasn't sure what had awakened him until he realized someone was standing near his bed. Very gingerly he moved his aching head to see who it was. "Oh it's you again," he remarked, seeing Captain Blake. "Where did you disappear to so fast?"

"It makes no matter where I be disappearin' to, matey. What matters is I be back, and I be ready to help ye take leave of this place. Ye has work to be doin', says I."

Michael sat up in bed, his eyes opening wide with surprise. "I have work to do, you say? What work? Wait a minute, you know who I am, don't you? Help me out here, friend. What's my name and how did I end up getting shot?"

"It's sorry I am indeed, laddie, but I be not allowed to discuss those things lost to your recollection. It be the decree of the higher authorities that ye find your memory on your own. Them be their very words."

Michael stared at him. "Higher authorities? What higher authorities. If you know who I am, Blake, for pity's sake, tell me. I'm wandering around in a fog here, and I need your help."

"Aye, matey, that be the truth. Ye do be needin' me help. And I'll be givin' ye me help, too. The first matter of business we be facin', is to be getting ye out of this here sick bay."

Michael threw up his hands. "In case you hadn't noticed, Blake. There's an armed guard at my door. Even if I did agree to leave the hospital with you, how do you propose we get by the guard? And so far as that goes, I'm not even sure I can get out of this bed—let alone pull off an escape in my condition."

"Leave everythin' to me, matey. I'll have ye out of this scurvy-infested dungeon faster than the peasants clear the courtyard at the king's command. There be a set of clothes hangin' in yonder closet, says I." Blake pointed to a closet next to the bathroom. "I'll be obliged if ye'll be slipping into them."

Michael took one look at the closet, then turned his attention back to the captain. "I have a gunshot wound to the head, Blake. You want me to get dressed and attempt an escape. Why, pray tell? It would seem to me that I'd be better off right here where I can get all the help I need."

Blake stood tall, folding his arms across his burly chest. "Ye has work to be doin', matey. Things that matter to ye be in a turmoil at the present, says I. If ye'll be risin' yer bones from that bed, I'll be obliged."

Something about Blake's words struck a chord with Michael. From deep in his subconscious mind, a voice seemed to cry out that things really were in turmoil in his life. He dropped the argument. Pulling back the covers, he slid his feet very gingerly to the floor. His head throbbed and the room spun wildly. "I don't know about this, Blake." he cautiously observed. "If you want me out of this hospital, you may just have to carry me out."

Blake laughed. "Sorry, matey, that cannot be done. I be a first-level angel, and first-level angels be not privy to such tasks as carrying mortals, says I."

Michael stared at the captain. Several things the fellow had said made little or no sense. The mention of a first-level angel thing was just one example. Michael decided to let it go, and since his head was clearing some, he made a stab at rising to his feet.

"Okay," he allowed. "I made it this far. Maybe I can do this after all." Grinning, he looked Blake right in the eye and added, "Says I."

Blake responded to his gesture with a grin of his own and a brief salute. Cautiously, Michael took a step toward the closet. "That went well," he avowed. He tried a second step, then a third. One deep breath, and he set out for the closet, arriving there somewhat dizzy, but still on his feet. "So far so good, Blake," he said, reaching for the knob and pulling the door open.

Michael stared into the open closet. Blake had told the truth about the clothes, but were these really his clothes? "What am I, some sort of cowboy?" he asked.

"No, matey, ye be not a cowboy. The lad who belonged to these clothes be the cowboy. His name be Rusty Dunkin, and he be one of those singing sorts, who puts on a show for folks in the evenings, says I. But he be your same size, matey. And the Davy Jones outfit ye be wearin' when ye came to this place be not the sort of clothes suitable for where ye be headed."

A second look into the closet revealed a diver's wetsuit hanging on the rack in a clear plastic bag. He guessed this must be what the captain was referring to as a Davy Jones outfit. Traces of what appeared to be blood near the top of the wetsuit could be seen through the plastic. "Is this wetsuit what I was wearing when I was shot?" he aked.

"Aye, matey, that be the case," the captain affirmed.

Michael looked at it closely. "What am I? A Navy Seal or something?"

"In due time, lad, ye'll be learnin' the answer to all these questions," the captain said patiently. "For now, asks I, just be trustin' me."

Michael reached to the top of the closet and retrieved a black Stetson hat from off the shelf. "Can you at least tell me what this cowboy singer's clothes are doing in my hospital room?"

Blake was quick with an affirmative nod. "The lad was in these quarters before ye arrived here, matey. Bleedin' ulcers in his stomach, says the doctor. One too many trips to the rum barrel, thinks I. They took him away to be put under the knife, and his clothes be forgotten in the rush of it all. Not that his clothes be left here by accident, ye be understandin'. Me matey, the honorable Mr. Gus, who be a second-level angel, had a finger in the matter, be it known."

Michael took a long hard look at Captain Blake. "First-level angels, second-level angels . . . what are you talking about, Blake?"

"Me meanin' will be clear to yer understandin' when the winds of fortune fill again the sails of your memory, matey. As for now, just be knowin' this, ye be in good hands with the likes of Mr. Gus lookin' after ye."

"I'm in good hands, eh?" Michael questioned cynically. "I've been shot in the head, can't remember who I am, and stand accused of being a drug dealer. Yep, sure sounds like I'm in good hands, all right." He looked back into the closet at the singer's clothes. There was a light jacket, a pair of Levis, a red western-style shirt, a pair of boots, and a leather belt with a buckle the size of post card. On the face of the buckle was the image of a long-horn bull's head. It was true that Michael had no memory of who he was or how he fit into society, but this much he knew for sure; these clothes did not match his lifestyle. "Are you sure these things will fit me, Blake?" he asked.

"Aye, matey. I be sure. It be part of the plan."

Michael caught a glimpse of his own image in a small mirror hanging on the inside of the closet door. He gasped at what he saw. The whole upper part of his head was covered with thick bandaging. "Oh my gosh!" he moaned. "I'm a mess. You can't expect me to walk out of this hospital with this thing on my head, Blake. It won't exactly help me slip unnoticed through the crowd, you know."

"That's what the hat be for, matey."

Michael glanced at the hat, still in his hand. Looking back to the mirror, he very carefully placed it on his head. He found by pulling the hat down as far as possible, it did a fair job of hiding the bandaging. Not that it didn't add to the throbbing in his head, because it most certainly did. But if he were to have any hope of leaving the hospital unnoticed, he'd just have to suffer the pain.

"Okay, partner," he conceded wryly. "Looks like I'm fixin' to become a pseudo-cowboy fer a spell. Ya reckon the boots 'ull fit?" His moment of lightheartedness was brought to an abrupt end as the door that led to the nurses' station opened. Michael spun around to see the blue-uniformed guard staring at him with a look of dumbfounded confusion.

"What's the problem, buddy?" the guard asked. "Why are you out of bed and what's with the hat? Do you need a nurse or something?"

CHAPTER 8

As the sun came up, Jenice rose and walked to the small window. To her surprise, she discovered something more than she had seen the night before. This time, instead of simply looking at miles of ocean, she was looking at the shoreline of a small island. She did a double take and couldn't believe her eyes. This was not just any island—it was the one. . . But how could that be possible? She rubbed her eyes, and looked again. Nothing changed, she was still looking at what seemed like an impossibility.

Even as she tried to grasp the reality of it all, she was distracted by the sound of her cabin door opening. Looking around, she fully expected to see Stuart Fox. She was wrong.

"Roy!" she gasped at seeing him enter the room. "What—how?"

Roy was holding a pistol. He quickly raised a finger to his lips quieting her. "Hurry, Jenice," he whispered excitedly. "Let's get out of here!"

Jenice hurriedly moved to the open door. "You've escaped?" she asked, keeping her voice low.

"Yeah. I overpowered Fox. He's tied and gagged in my cabin."

"You took his gun from him?"

"Yeah, I figured it might come in handy. We've got to find a way off this yacht. If we can just reach the small island, we'll have a sporting chance of eluding these guys."

Roy took Jenice by the hand, and the two of them slipped out the door. They quickly moved to the top of the stairs. Glancing over the railing, he satisfied himself there was no one in sight. "I'm sure there'll be at least one of them at the wheel," he said. "I think we can slip up on him unnoticed, just so long as we don't encounter anyone else along the way. I'm hoping they're all in the mess hall chowing down on breakfast. Come on," he said, moving down the short flight of stairs.

At the bottom everything still looked good. Slowly Roy inched toward the control cabin, with Jenice close on his heels. When they reached the doorway to the cabin, Jenice peeked over Roy's shoulder to see a single man at the wheel. It was Max Yorty. Roy made a move to step inside, gun drawn. Jenice grabbed his arm. "No!" she whispered. "This guy is mine."

Without giving Roy the chance to argue, she stepped around him and came in full sight of Max. She put on her best smile. "Hello, handsome," she said seductively. "I was hoping to find you alone. With those other guys out of the way, maybe you and I can get a little better acquainted. What do you think?"

Max's eyes shot open wide. His chin dropped and he stared as she slowly moved closer. "What do you say, Max? Wouldn't you like to get a little better acquainted with me?"

Max's mouth worked, but no words came out. He glanced at his gun laying on a small table on the opposite side of the cabin. Jenice stopped right in front of him. "That's really a nice ponytail you have there, Max." She grinned and very slowly reached out a hand as if to stroke his hair. "You must use Pantene to get that luster."

Max stiffened and moved his head abruptly back. It was too late. The poor man never knew what hit him. Grabbing a handful of hair, Jenice pulled his face downward even as her knee shot up to meet it halfway. He didn't so much as let out a groan before hitting the floor, out cold.

"Maybe you should think twice before calling me 'a broad' again," she said sharply. "I detest that wretched term."

"Come on," Roy called. "Let's get a lifeboat in the water before anyone else walks in on us."

The coast was clear, and they made it to the lifeboat with no problem. But before they had a chance to lower it, Jenice caught sight of a movement out of the corner of her eye. With no time to warn Roy, she ducked behind the boat, out of sight. A split second later, she heard the culprit call out. "Hey, you! What are you doing there?!"

"Don't use the gun; it will alert the others," Jenice whispered. "Lure him over here where I can reach him."

Roy held the gun behind his back. "I—I was just getting a breath of fresh air," he told the man. "I found my door unlocked this morning, and I figured no one would mind."

The fellow put a hand to his mouth and squinted at Roy. "Yer door was unlocked, you say?"

"Yes, that's right. I just figured since I've been behaving myself, I was being rewarded. That is right, isn't it?"

The fellow looked around and seeing no one else, he started at a slow pace toward Roy. "I'm not all that sure," he said. "I think you'd better come along with me. We'll ask Max or Lefty about it. They should know what to do with you."

Jenice held her breath for fear the man wouldn't get close enough. Fortunately, he did. He moved very slowly, but he kept coming. When at last he was within reach, she made her move. Jumping from behind the lifeboat, she placed a solid kick to his midsection. Grabbing an arm, she twisted it hard behind his back and threw a neck lock on him with her other arm. Before he could recover his senses, Roy had the gun hard against the crew member's face. "Not one sound," he said. "Not so much as a sigh." The man froze in place like a marble statue.

"Very good," Roy said, using his free hand to release the canvas tie-down strap which had secured the lifeboat in place. "Now, the three of us are going to get in the boat. And we're going to do it with no objections, got that, friend?" The culprit gave a frightened nod. "Okay, you can let him go, Jenice. I think he's a wise enough fellow to know what's best for him."

Jenice released the man and Roy forced him into the boat. Jenice stepped in next, and pressed the button on the automatic launch system. Slowly, the boat lowered into the water.

Roy handed the gun to Jenice. "You keep our boy entertained," he said. "I'll row us ashore."

Quietly, Roy slid the oars into the water. Using his foot, he shoved off from the yacht and began rowing. Jenice glanced over her shoulder at the island. It was only a few hundred yards away. "Over there, Roy," she said, pointing off to her right. "It looks like a cove. That might be a good place to put in."

"Yeah, I see it. That's where we'll head."

"Wha—what do you plan on doing with me?" the frightened hostage asked nervously.

"That's a good question," Roy contemplated. "What can we do with you, my good man?"

"Can you swim?" Jenice asked.

"Yeah, sure. Are you gonna turn me loose?"

"Well now I'm not sure," Jenice responded. "If I do turn you loose, what exactly will you do?"

"I won't say nothin' to them about where you went. Ya got my word on it, lady. I won't say nothin'."

Roy gave Jenice an inquisitive look. "You think it's a good idea turning him loose?" he asked. "I realize he says he'll keep his mouth shut and all, but . . ."

"They're going to find out we've gone anyway, Roy. And where else could we go but to the island? Turning this guy loose won't make all that much difference. And, what else can we do with him. He'll just be in our way on the island." Jenice gave Roy a quick wink. "The only other choice is to kill him."

"Kill me?!" he shrieked. "No, no! I beg of you! Let me go! I won't say nothin', I promise."

Jenice leaned down and picked up one of the life jackets from a pile of several on the floor of the boat. "Here," she said, handing it to the man. "It's your lucky day; I'm not in the mood for any more killing. We'll put you overboard when we get a little closer to the island."

*　*　*

"What's the problem, buddy?" Seeing Michael out of bed, standing near the open closet door, the guard moved closer. "Do you need a nurse or something?"

Michael quickly tossed the hat back into the closet and closed the door. "Uh, no," he managed to respond. "I'm fine. I was looking for the bathroom and wandered into the closet by mistake. I'll be okay now that I have it figured out."

"You're sure?" the guard pressed suspiciously. "I can get you some help . . ."

"No, really, I'm fine. I just need a little privacy. You know how it is."

"Whatever you say, pal. Give us a holler if you change your mind."

Michael breathed a sigh of relief as the guard stepped out and closed the door. As he turned to face the captain again, a strange thought came to mind. "Why didn't that guard say anything about you being in my room, Blake? Darwell left strict orders that no one was to be in here."

Blake grinned. "I be supposin' the guard didn't notice me, matey."

"How could he not notice you, you were standing in plain sight for all the world to see. Something funny is going on here, Blake. I don't know what it is, but I don't like it."

"Ye'll be understandin' it all when the time comes, laddie. Ye has me word on it."

"When the time comes," Michael echoed with disgust. "And until that time I'm just supposed to trust you, is that it?"

"Aye, matey. And I won't be lettin' ye down."

Anger filled Michael's mind at his lost memory. Captain Blake was obviously playing games with him, which he didn't like one tiny bit. *Trust me,* Blake kept saying. Michael didn't want to trust him. Michael wanted to hear some positive answers to the pool of questions swimming around in his head. But—that obviously wasn't going to be the case. So, there was little else to do but trust the fellow. Disgusting as the thought seemed, that's how things were.

Michael checked the door one last time to be certain the guard was outside, then he returned to the closet. He took out the shirt and put it on. Next came the jeans. As he reached for the boots, something else caught his eye. It looked like a shoe box. He picked it up and slid off the lid. Inside the box he found a small pocket knife, a ring of keys, a handkerchief, seventy-three cents in change, and a pocket watch. "What do we have here, Blake?" he asked. "Are these my things, or do they belong to the cowboy?"

"They be your belongings, matey."

Michael searched the box to see if he had missed anything that might help identify who he was. There was nothing. No wallet, no papers, nothing. He was sure whoever shot him didn't want any identifying articles left on his person. And he was just as sure they had planted the drugs on him as incriminating evidence.

He examined the watch more closely. It seemed strikingly familiar. He pressed the stem opening the watch. To his surprise, he discovered a woman's picture on the inside cover. The image of her face leapt out at him. He knew this woman, but why couldn't he put a name with her face? Such a beautiful face. So beautiful, it could only be described as the face of an angel. For nearly a minute he stared at her features, desperately trying to remember. It was no use. He finally closed the watch and slid it in his pants pocket along with the other items taken from the shoe box.

He finished dressing. Then gritting his teeth against the pain, he returned the hat to his head. "Okay, Blake," he stated calmly. "The ball's in your court. How do you plan on getting that guard away from my door?"

"I'll not be removin' the guard, says I. I'll be takin' ye out the back way."

"Back way?" Michael asked, taking a long look around the room. "There is no back way, Blake. Not unless you mean that window over there."

Blake nodded. "'Do I go out through the window?' asks ye. 'Yes,' answers I. 'You do go out through the window to the ledge you'll be findin' there.' The ledge be wide as a pirate's plank, perfectly suited for your escape, matey."

"What?!" Michael gasped, fighting to keep his voice down so as not to attract the attention of the guard. "You want me to climb out on a ledge in my condition?"

"Aye, that be the plan."

Michael shook his head in disbelief. "Do you mind my asking what floor we're on?"

* * *

Roy maneuvered the boat around to line up with the cove inlet. When they were within a hundred feet or so, Jenice spoke. "Okay, buster, here's where you get off. Now just remember, you gave us your word not to say a thing about where we made off to."

"I won't say nothin'!" the frightened man shot back. "My lips are closed tighter than Max's rum locker."

"Go on, get out," Jenice said, with a sideward nod of her head toward the water. The man put up no argument. He hit the water with a loud splash and was backpedaling his way toward the yacht before the last spray of water droplets fell back in. Jenice would have found it funny if it hadn't been for the constant ache in her heart over Michael.

Minutes later, Roy put the boat ashore. "I can't believe our luck at having those guys lay anchor next to this very island," Jenice exclaimed as they headed for the cover of the rainforest. "This is the same island where Michael and I ended up when we fell overboard from the luxury liner, *The Wandering Star.*"

"And the same island where I was covering the story of an impending storm. That's why I was here in the helicopter and was able to fly you to the mainland for medical help with your concussion." He stopped and smiled at Jenice. "And just for your information, those guys didn't anchor here by chance. I persuaded them to come here."

"You did? But why?"

"It's simple, really. We needed an escape plan, and I figured since we were somewhat familiar with this island, it was our best shot. So . . . I simply used my reporter skills to convince Mr. Fox that you had secretly confided in me where the map is hidden—right here on this island."

"Stuart bought that?" Jenice asked, surprised. "Your cabin was bugged, Roy. He heard every word we said, and I never mentioned the map being hidden on this island."

"Piece of cake, Jenice. I convinced him we knew the bug was there and were communicating by notes."

"Which we conveniently destroyed before he came to our cabin, right?"

Roy shrugged. "What can I say? The man was just greedy enough to buy any story he thought would lead him to that map. Fortunately, I remembered the exact location of this island from the day I was here in the helicopter. I gave him the coordinates and he had the crew sail here during the night."

"Interesting," Jenice remarked. "And just when did all this skul- duggery take place?"

Roy laughed. "Stuart showed up in my cabin not fifteen minutes after escorting you away last night. You can probably guess his pitch. He has you for a hostage now, and unless I open up—you end up in the drink."

Jenice nodded. "I figured that was coming."

"Then, when Stuart showed up at my cabin this morning, I was ready for him. Took him by complete surprise. I gagged him and tied him up with strips of bed sheeting. I found the key to cabin eight in his pocket and surmised that's where he had taken you. I guess luck was on our side. Did I do good, or what, lady?"

"That all depends, Roy. On whether they find us or not. They're bound to figure out we're on the island."

"Knowing we're on the island and finding us are two different things, Jenice. This island is a jungle. You could hide a herd of elephants on it with a little luck. The way I figure, if we can stay ahead of these guys long enough, they'll give up and hightail it out of here."

"What makes you think that?" Jenice questioned.

"It's quite simple, my dear lady," Roy laughed. "These guys won't stay in any one spot for very long. Too much chance of the law catching up with them. All we have to do is hold out a few days, a week at most and they'll turn tail, I guarantee it. Once they're gone, we can figure how to signal for help. Now what do you say we move inland where we can get ourselves lost in a rainforest. They'll come here looking for us. We might as well make ourselves as hard to find as possible."

Jenice sighed. Roy was right, of course. Their only chance was to move deeper into the island and do their best to stay hidden.

* * *

"We be on the fifth floor, matey," Captain Blake informed Michael. "But ye can set your mind at ease. Me friend Gus tells me he won't be allowin' no accident to your person, the gunshot to your head being the one exception to the matter."

Michael let out a low whistle. "I'm sorry, Blake, but at the moment I'm hard pressed to put a lot of trust in your friend Gus." Walking to the window, Michael found it unlatched. And of all things, there were no bars on the window; all hospitals have bars on the upper-floor windows, he thought. But if there had been bars on this window, they had been removed. More of this Gus's doing, he suspected. He opened the window and glanced out at the ledge. "Wide as a pirate's plank, you say, eh, Blake? I doubt many pirate's planks are this high up, and most usually have water under them. You're certain this is the only way out for me?"

"I be certain, matey. And I be certain me friend Gus will be keepin' you safe. Be not forgetting, it was Gus who spoiled the black-guard's aim that fired the ball at your head."

Michael looked again at the narrow ledge. Common sense told him to return to the room and forget this whole foolish idea of escape. Especially since his head wound left him with something less than the full sense of balance needed to walk a plank-size ledge. But that nagging voice from somewhere deep inside told him he had little other choice. Easing himself out the window, he put one foot on the ledge. Very carefully, he brought the other foot into position. Leaning back hard against the wall, he dared to look down five stories at the concrete patio below where he stood.

"Which way do I go, Blake?" he asked hoarsely.

"Move to your left, matey. And I be suggestin' ye not be lookin' down."

"I already did look down, Blake. You're cruel, you know that. Here I am about to fall five stories to a certain death, and you won't even tell me what name I'll have on my headstone."

"You'll not be fallin' matey. Ye has me word on it."

"Yeah, right," Michael said, inching his left foot forward along the ledge. Very slowly, he shifted his weight and brought the right foot along to meet the left. In this same manner he kept inching one step after another until he had reached the first window along the way. He gave it a gentle shove, only to realize it was closed and locked from the inside. Besides, it had a set of bars protecting it. "What do I do now, Blake?" he grumbled. "I can't get in this window."

"Wrong window, matey. The window ye'll be escapin' through be two more down the way."

"Great! Just what I wanted to hear. I'm only a third of the way there," Michael responded sarcastically, then, drawing a deep breath, he started moving along the ledge again.

At last he passed the second window. Only one third of the way remained. The process was slow, but at least his confidence was increasing with each step. After what seemed an eternity, he reached the third window. To his great relief, this one was open. And no bars. He glanced inside the room. It appeared to be empty.

"Are ye planning on standing there all mornin' drinking in the view, matey, or do ye plan on coming inside so we can hoist anchor and get this voyage under way?"

Michael was dumbfounded to see Blake already inside the room. "How did you get around me?" he asked sharply. "You were behind me, Blake." Michael closed his eyes and leaned hard against the wall for several seconds. "Never mind," he said at length. "I wouldn't understand it even if you did explain." Catching his breath, he stepped through the window into the room.

"The outside hall be empty at this very time," Blake quickly pointed out. "I'll be obliged if ye'll not be dragging anchor, matey."

"You've already checked the hall?" Michael asked, shaking his head. "Why am I not surprised?" Hurrying to the door, Michael cracked it slightly. The room opened onto a hallway and Blake was right—it was empty at the moment. Easing into the hall, Michael spotted an elevator at the far end. He moved quickly to it and pressed the down button. Nervously, he waited. At last the light came on, indicating the car had reached the fifth floor. The doors opened and he quickly stepped inside. Pressing a finger to the button marked Lobby, he held his breath. The doors closed and the car began its descent. On the third floor, it stopped and two elderly ladies got on. He pulled the brim of his hat down a little tighter and was glad when they paid him no mind.

Moments later, the car reached the level of the main lobby. The two ladies stepped out with Michael right behind. They headed for a nearby gift shop; he made a beeline for the exit doors. Once outside, he looked around for Blake. The fellow was nowhere to be seen. That just had to be the strangest man Michael had ever run into. At least, the strangest he could remember running into, he surmised with the slightest hint of a grin. But of all the times for Blake to disappear, what was Michael supposed to do now? Even though he had a feeling he was needed somewhere, he had no idea where that could be. He had just assumed that Blake would lead him wherever he was supposed to go. Should he go left or right? What was he supposed to do, flip a coin?

Then he heard the captain's voice. "Go left, matey. I'll be with ye all the way." Michael closed his eyes in amazement. It had happened again. Without the slightest explanation, he heard the voice of an invisible man telling him which way to go. He didn't argue. What was the use? He headed to the left as quickly as his legs would allow, rapidly distancing himself from the hospital.

* * *

"The Evening Star Celestial Dining Room?" Samantha said, staring skeptically at the entrance to the place Jason had brought her. "This is where your friend, the head chef, works, isn't it?"

"This is the place, Sam. And Daniel is your ticket home."

Samantha hesitated. "But Daniel's a chef, Jason. How can he offer us transportation back to our own galaxy?"

"Elementary, my dear sweetheart. Daniel does catering all over dozens of galaxies. We'll simply hitch a ride on one of his delivery routes. I know Daniel won't mind going a few million miles out of his way to take us home. Think about it, my cute little wife. He's a fellow chef. There's nothing one chef won't do for another chef. It's an unwritten code."

Samantha pulled Jason into a warm embrace and tender kiss. "Wow! What was that for?" he asked smiling.

"That's for being my knight in shining armor, Mr. Hackett. Just get me home to Michael, and I'll never say bad things about you being a chef again."

CHAPTER 9

Max groaned and rubbed his throbbing head. "What did that broad hit me with?" he moaned, struggling to his feet. "She's gonna pay for this. Oh is she gonna pay!"

Max glanced at the open ocean surrounding the yacht. It was calm and no other ships were in sight. Since the yacht was anchored and all power down, he didn't worry much about leaving the helm unmanned. He staggered out of the cabin trying to get his bearings. Where could the woman be? He certainly didn't want her jumping out at him from behind some object. What was that sound? He paused to listen more closely. It was coming from the upper deck. It was a pounding sound, like someone trying to send out a signal. Gathering his strength, he rushed up the stairs.

The sound was coming from cabin six. That's the cabin where Stuart put that Roy fellow when he brought him onboard yesterday morning. Max tried the door. It was unlocked, so he pushed it open. There he spotted Stuart Fox, bound and gagged, and kicking against the cabin wall with all his might. Max was beside him in an instant, removing the gag and loosening the cotton strips used to bind him. "What's happened here, boss?" Max asked tensely.

"A double cross, that's what's happened!" Stuart snapped back angrily as he shot to his feet. "No one double crosses Stuart Fox and lives to tell about it!"

"Double cross? What double cross, boss? This Roy character, you mean?"

"That's exactly who I mean, Yorty. I should have known his story didn't add up. Especially when his bogus short-range tracking system wouldn't let us locate Michael's boat until after they'd abandoned the sight of the dive."

Max looked doubtful. "When they were lookin' for the gold, ya mean?"

Stuart threw up both hands. "Yes! Yes! Yes!" he yelled. "Jenkins didn't want us knowing where the gold is. That's why he came up with that useless tracking system. He used us, Max. He caught me completely off guard; I never saw it coming. We've got to stop him before he takes the girl and hightails it for that island out there. That's where she has the map hidden. At least that's what Roy said when he convinced me to sail here last night."

Stuart paused to look at Max's face. "Where'd you get the shiners?" he pressed. "You been in a fight?"

Max turned to look at himself in the mirror just behind where he was standing. To his immediate displeasure, he realized he had two black eyes. "That stupid broad did this!" he growled. "When I get my hands on her . . ."

"The woman?!" Stuart shot back. He slapped a hand to his brow. "She's free, too?! We got to find them, Yorty. Before they find a way of reaching that island. If they get there, we're in deep trouble."

"Man overboard!" came a cry from somewhere on the lower deck. "Somebody give me a hand gettin' him on board!"

Stuart was out the door in a flash. "Who is it?" he called out, leaning over the railing to watch the rescue efforts.

"It's Sammy!" one of the men shouted back. "He says that fellow Roy Jenkins and the woman done this to him."

* * *

Michael glanced at his watch. It was a quarter to ten. He pulled the collar of his jacket a little more tightly around his neck to help block the damp chill of the morning air. He walked quickly, hoping to put as much distance as possible between himself and the hospital.

The next time Michael paused to check his watch again, an hour and a half had passed. For the first time, he realized he was hungry. And no wonder, considering the fresh smell of fried bacon coming from the small cafe he had stopped in front of. The scent was tantalizing. Reaching into his pocket, he removed what change he had. Seventy-three cents. He couldn't buy much of a breakfast with that. Maybe a small carton of milk at best. *Milk,* he thought. What a letdown. Never had anything smelled so good as that bacon did at this minute. There was no way of knowing when he had eaten last. What wouldn't he give for a five-dollar bill right about now?

Out of nowhere, Michael heard the voice again. No question about it, it was Captain Blake. "Check the pocket watch, matey, and be quick about it. It be holdin' the key to yer breakfast, says I."

Michael looked first to the left, then to the right. He wasn't the least bit surprised to see no one there. By this time, he was growing used to these strange proceedings. Not that he had the slightest inkling how they were happening, but it was becoming easier to accept them.

The pocket watch? He thought. *What possible reason could Blake have for wanting me to check my pocket watch?* There was only one way to find out. Michael removed the watch and opened it. He looked again at picture inside. The face of an angel, and a face that seemed to hold the key to unlock the dark prison holding his memory captive in its walls. Still, for another long moment, the key remained just outside his reach. Then, suddenly, a faint glimmer of light penetrated the blackness, and he knew. The woman in the picture was someone who loved him deeply. The watch had been a gift from her.

"Yes!" he shouted as the memory came clearer. "She gave me the watch because I loved to travel all over the world. She wanted me to have it as a memento to remind me of her wherever I was, whenever I wanted to know the time."

He looked again at her picture, and a name exploded into his mind. "Sam! Your name is Sam! And you're—you're my sister!" With an exuberant shout, he cried out another name. "Michael! Michael Allen!" In his excitement, he slammed at the air with a clenched fist. "That's me!" he shouted again. "I'm Michael Allen!"

He looked at the watch and burst out laughing. "Way to go, Sam!" he cried. "You told me when you gave me this watch the time would come when I'd need what you had hidden inside. Well, big sister, you hit that one on the head. If I ever needed your gift, now is the time."

He dug a thumbnail under the edge of Samantha's picture and pulled it away from the watch. Behind the picture lay two folded green bills. As he looked at the bills, Samantha's words came back clearly, the words she'd spoken when she gave him the watch: *Never touch this money, little brother. Not until you find yourself in a situation where there's no other way out. Then you can use the money with my blessings. And when you do, remember to think of your big sister and all the times she bailed you out as a kid.*

Michael struggled to remember the last time he had seen Sam. Where was she now? But these things still refused to surface from the guarded channels of his memory. He consoled himself that at least he knew who she was, and he knew who he was. And now he had all the money he needed for a wonderful breakfast of bacon and eggs.

"Thanks, Sam, wherever you are," he said, a smile beaming on his face. "What a great sister you are." Removing two one-hundred-dollar bills from the watch, he returned Samantha's picture to its rightful place. Then, shoving the money in his pocket, he stepped inside the cafe.

It was a small place and there were no other customers at the moment. A woman stood behind the counter, wearing a typical waitress apron, but for some reason she seemed out of place. At first, Michael couldn't figure why. Then it struck him. Beneath her apron, she wore a stylish business suit—something that definitely seemed out of place. She was smiling.

In the kitchen behind the open serving counter, Michael could see the cook and he couldn't help thinking the cook seemed out of place, as well. It wasn't so much the way he looked, but more the way he went about preparing things in the kitchen. He seemed a little clumsy to be an experienced cook.

But the hungry feeling in Michael's stomach was not about to be ignored, so he shrugged off all questions about the cook and waitress, and took a seat on one of the counter stools.

"May I help you?" the waitress asked, stepping in front of where he was seated.

Michael started to remove his hat, as was his custom when he was indoors. Suddenly he stopped. If he removed the hat, the bandage would show and perhaps bring questions he'd rather not answer. Still, if he didn't remove the hat, it was a show of bad manners, which was something that bothered Michael a great deal. The waitress's next comment completely surprised him.

"Go ahead, Michael, take off the hat. There's no need to hide the bandage in here."

He gawked at her. Was he supposed to know this woman? She obviously knew him. But—even if she did know him, how could she possible know about his head wound? There were just so many things he couldn't remember, and Michael was growing more frustrated and perplexed by the minute.

"Don't worry about not remembering, Michael. You're among friends," she continued and the warmth of her smile eased Michael's fears. "How about some breakfast? That is what you came in here for, isn't it?"

"Uh, yeah," he stammered, not understanding what was happening but too grateful to argue about it. "The bacon smells great. And maybe a couple of eggs, over-easy, and some toast."

"How about a short stack of hot cakes to top it off?" the waitress smiled.

"That does sound good. Add the hot cakes, too."

"I think we can accommodate that," she said, turning to pick up the plate of food the cook had placed on the counter. Michael couldn't believe it. He had scarcely placed his order, and the cook had the plate filled and ready for him. It was just one more mystery to add to the string of others. Michael removed his hat and shoved it underneath the barstool where he was seated, then turned to the plate of food before him. The bacon was a little too crisp, the eggs were definitely overcooked, and the hotcakes . . . Well, suffice it to say he had seen better-looking hot cakes than these. But at the moment, he didn't care. It all smelled great. And as it turned out, it didn't taste half bad, if only because he was so hungry.

Michael looked up as the waitress placed a large glass of milk on the counter in front of him. He noticed she was also holding a set of drawing pencils and a sketch pad. "Here," she said, handing them to Michael. "When you finish your breakfast, you can use these to draw her face."

"Her face?" Michael asked, surprised. "Whose face?"

The woman's smile grew even warmer. "That pocket knife you found among your personal items . . . do you still have it with you?"

Michael reached in his pocket and removed the knife, which he held up for her to see. "This one, you mean?"

"That's the one," she affirmed. "Where did you get it, Michael?"

"I—I'm not sure where I got it," he confessed.

"It'll come to you, I promise. Now eat your breakfast."

Michael took a long look at the waitress. "I don't mean to be rude," he said. "But there are some things I'd really like to ask, if you don't mind."

"Ask away, Michael. I'll be glad to answer anything the higher authorities will allow."

"Uh, yeah," Michael said, considering that term again. "We wouldn't want any questions answered the 'higher authorities' wouldn't like, would we?"

She smiled but said nothing. "My first question," Michael said, "is about an old sea captain named Horatio Symington Blake. Am I off base assuming you know the captain?"

She removed her apron and cap, tossing them onto a shelf under the counter. "Let me help you out, Michael," she said. "My name's Maggie. And no, you've never met me, if that's what you're wondering. But that doesn't mean I don't know you, because I do. I know about your head injury, I know about your memory loss, and I know that everything is going to be fine with you. And yes, I do know Captain Blake. He and I work for the same team, so to speak."

"Uh huh, I thought so. And the cook, let me guess. His name is Gus, right? I heard Captain Blake mention the name Gus, so I just figured . . ."

Maggie nodded her head. "His name is Gus, and he's one of us, Michael."

Michael pressed his luck. "I don't suppose you'd care to fill me in on how all these strange things keep happening, would you, Maggie?"

Maggie reached out and took the pocket knife from Michael. "The higher authorities have made it clear that we can't force your memory back," she explained. "And before you ask, the higher authorities are what you might think of as my supervisors. Mine, Captain Blake's, Gus's, all of ours. That's about all I can tell you about

them, Michael. But take my word for it, when they say something—
it's best to listen." She lay the knife next to his plate. "They have
authorized us to use a few familiar items to help bring back your
memory. Such as the pocket watch, and this little knife. Go ahead
and eat your breakfast. And while you do, keep thinking about this
knife. It will bring back a memory, I promise."

Michael glanced down at the knife. When he looked up again,
Maggie was gone. He made a quick check of the kitchen; Gus was
gone, too. Michael rested his head in his hand. It was bad enough
having a sea captain who kept him guessing what might be coming
next; now this waitress and cook had joined ranks with the captain.

"I think I know now how Alice must have felt when she was in
Wonderland," he groaned to himself. "So help me, if a big rabbit with
a pocket watch shows up . . ." He shook his head. There was no use
in questioning something he had no way of understanding anyway.
He glanced at the food on his plate. No sense in letting that go to
waste, either. He picked up his fork and resumed eating hungrily.

All through breakfast, he kept staring at the little knife. At first,
he remembered nothing. But after a while, the image of a woman's
face began forming in his mind. She was standing in front of the
Eiffel tower in Paris, France. Yes, that's where she was. And she had
given him a gift. It was the pocket knife.

He struggled to remember her name. It refused to come to him.
But even without a name, he could visualize her face. Every tiny
detail of her face. He grabbed the sketch pad, and taking a pencil
from the drawing set, began to sketch her image. Minutes later, he
had a perfect likeness of her face on the paper.

* * *

Detective Darwell pulled the last potato chip from the bag and
bit into it. Crumpling the empty bag, he tossed it into the already
overflowing wastebasket at the edge of his desk. Then he walked to
the water cooler in the corner of his office, pulled out a paper cup,
and filled it. Downing it in one gulp, he crumpled the cup and glared
across the room at the janitor who was cleaning the window on his
office door. "Why is it we can't get some decent water in this place?!

This stuff tastes like it was dredged from the bottom of a swamp. You!" He snapped at the janitor. "What's your name?"

The janitor looked back at him nervously. "It's Aaron, sir. Aaron James."

"Well, Aaron James, do you suppose it would be asking too much to get this bottle of swill out of my office and get me some digestible drinking water? And get me a new water cooler while you're at it. One that keeps the water cold."

"Yes sir, I'll see to it someone orders one right away."

"You'll get one ordered? Tell me something, Aaron. Have you ever seen an order filled in this place in less than a month? No, of course you haven't, because it never happens." Darwell waved his arm wildly at the man. "Get out there and find me a water cooler now! I don't care where you find one, just find it. I want some decent drinking water in this office before it's locked up for the night. Got it, Aaron?"

"Yes sir, yes sir," Aaron said, nodding his head three or four times while backing out of the office. "Right away sir." He turned and hurried out.

Darwell threw the paper cup at the wastebasket, but missed. Ignoring it, he picked up the ringing phone. "Darwell here."

"Yes, sir, Detective Darwell? This is Officer Fred Duffy. There's something I need to report."

"Fred? What are you doing at the phone? You're supposed to be guarding a prisoner, aren't you?"

In a shaky voice, Officer Duffy's forced out the words. "That's what I need to report to you, Detective. The guy's gone. He just vanished from his room."

"Vanished from his room?!" Darwell shouted into the phone. "People don't just vanish, Duffy. I distinctly remember leaving you to guard his door. How did he get out?"

"I swear, I don't know how he got out. I never left my post for one second."

Darwell dropped the phone to his side and stared stiffly at the ceiling for several seconds. Then moving the phone back to his mouth, he barked, "I had a surveillance camera installed in that room, Duffy. Get the tape out of it and find us a room with a player where we can look at it. I'll be at the hospital in twenty minutes. You got that, Duffy?"

"Yes, sir, Detective. I'll get right on it."

Darwell slammed down the phone and grabbed his overcoat from the back of his chair. "Imbeciles!" he grumbled on his way out the door. "I'm working with nothing but imbeciles."

* * *

Stuart Fox slammed his hand against the side of the yacht. "Blast it, Max! How did we let those two get away? Make the boat ready, we're going ashore. I'm not letting a fortune in sunken gold slip through my fingers, not when we're this close to finding it. And besides, I have a score to settle with a Mr. Roy Jenkins. No one double crosses Stuart Fox and lives to tell about it."

An evil grin crossed Max's face. "I got a score to settle, too, boss. You can have Roy Jenkins. The broad is mine."

"Have all the fun you want, Max. I couldn't care less. But for now, get the boat ready. Leave Lefty in charge here. It'll just be you and me going ashore. The rest of the men have no idea what's going on. They think everything is moving along according to plan. I'd just as soon leave them thinking that way. It'll mean less problems for us."

"Yeah, boss, I gotcha. And if we do learn where the gold is, a two-way split beats the other option, right?"

CHAPTER 10

Michael drank down the last of his milk and sat the glass back down on the counter, then looked around for someone who might take the money for his bill. Maggie and Gus were nowhere to be seen, nor was there anyone else in the cafe. Then he noticed it. The check was lying on the counter in front of his plate. Maggie must have left it there without his noticing. He picked it up. It was marked *Paid*.

"Why not?" he said with a baffled grin on his face. "It fits with everything else that's been filling up my day so far."

Putting on his hat, Michael stepped outside the cafe to find himself face to face with Captain Blake. "Oh there you are," he observed. "I was wondering when you'd show up again."

"It's sorry I be about the quality of breakfast," the captain responded. "Me friend Gus is a man of many talents, says I. But cookin' be not one of them."

"Look, Blake," Michael exclaimed. "How about we cut to the chase here? If you have something to tell me that will help get my memory back, just spit it out, okay? I'm getting tired of this game we're playing. Especially since I have zilch to say about the rules."

"Aye, matey, if it's wind ye be wantin' in yer sails, it's wind I'll be providin'. If ye'll be so kind as to be crossin' the street, there be somethin' I wishes ye to see in the window of yonder shop."

Michael looked in the direction Captain Blake was pointing. On the far side of the street he spotted a shop with a large sign on the window. It read MISS ALISSA'S BOOKS. Not knowing what to expect, but at the same time not wanting to miss the slightest chance of shedding some light on his dilemma, Michael immediately crossed the street. There, in the window of the store, a large poster caught his eye. It was an advertisement for a new book release. The title of the book was *The Man Who Loved Diamonds*. But it wasn't the title that had caught Michael's eye. It was the author's picture, shown in the upper right corner of the poster. She was an attractive young woman whose name was listed as Alexis Jenee. For a long moment, Michael stared at her picture. This was the third time a woman's face had tugged at his memory. The first was the picture in his pocket watch, who he later learned was his sister. The second was the face brought to mind by the little knife, the face he had drawn on the scratch pad, which was now tucked safely away in his shirt pocket. This woman on the poster seemed less personal to him than the others, but he was certain he had met her at some time in the past.

Stepping inside the store, he walked to the shelf where her book was on display. Picking up a copy, he thumbed through the pages, reading brief passages here and there. It was a detective novel, and strangely her main character shared Michael's exact name. The fictional Michael Allen was depicted as a carefree freelance detective who loved seeking out and solving a good mystery. This particular story took Michael to the Austrian Alps, where he became deeply involved in a plot concerning a fortune in stolen diamonds.

Michael turned to the back of the book. The inside back jacket cover displayed the same picture of the author he had seen on the poster. Beneath the picture was a brief personal description and a listing of five previous best-sellers. Then he noticed the author had listed an e-mail address. Maybe this was the reason Captain Blake had directed him to this store. Maybe he was meant to find this address.

The captain was nowhere in sight at the moment so Michael couldn't ask for sure about this, but it stood to reason, if he knew this author—chances were she might be able to help him recover some of his memory. He took the book to the counter and purchased it.

* * *

Detective Darwell strained to catch every detail of the video tape from the hospital room. He watched it twice, and then watched it a third time just to be sure he hadn't missed anything. "What idiot left a set of clothes in this guy's room?!" he barked. "And what is the man trying to pull, talking to a Captain Blake who doesn't exist? What's he up to, Duffy? This one's got me baffled."

"Maybe we have a nutcake here," Officer Duffy suggested.

"I don't buy it, slick. The guy knows exactly what it is he's up to. He knew the camera was there, I'd bet on it. The memory loss is a fake, too. It's a trick to throw us off the track."

Darwell stood abruptly and shoved a finger to the off button on the VCR. "I want this guy!" he growled. "He's part of the drug ring I've been tracking for months now, I feel it in my gut. This one will lead me to the whole ring, Duffy. I want an electronic picture of him cut from the video tape. And I want it in the hands of every squad car patrol in the city. Someone's got to recognize this guy. I mean that black hat alone should be a dead giveaway. Who does he think he is? Clint Black?"

"I'm on it, Detective. The picture will be in every patrol car in an hour."

Darwell spun to face Duffy, a finger pointed straight in his face. "Make that half an hour, slick! Not one second longer!"

* * *

As Michael stepped out of the bookstore, he noticed a taxi approaching. Stepping into the street, he hailed it down. "Gus?" he mused aloud, recognizing the driver. "You're a cabbie now?"

"Aye, laddie, that he be," Captain Blake answered from the back seat. "And a better cabbie he be, than a cook, says I."

"Get in, pal," Gus grumbled. "And pay no mind to the captain's sarcasm. Three hundred years hauntin' a hunk of lava in the Caribbean has left the guy with an attitude."

"Three hundred years of what?" Michael asked. Then throwing up both hands, he added, "Never mind, I'm probably better off not knowing. Can I assume the cab is for my benefit?"

Gus nodded. "Yep. Get in and I'll take ya to a place where ya can send off that e-mail. That is what ya have in mind, isn't it?"

Michael nodded his head and stepped into the cab, taking a seat next to Captain Blake. "I won't ask how you know that," he said, closing the door. "It's obvious you know everything that's going on here and just as obvious that you're not going to fill me in. So is the meter running on this hack, or is this trip on the house the same as breakfast?"

"It's on the house, pal, but considerin' we're only goin' a few blocks—that's not savin' ya a bunch anyhow."

Sure enough, Gus brought the taxi to a stop just blocks away. Michael glanced out the window to see that Gus had pulled up in front of a place called Copymasters. "Let me guess," Michael said. "I can send my e-mail out from this place, right?"

"They send e-mails, pal," Gus responded. "Among other things."

Michael opened the door and stepped out of the taxi. Before closing the door, he looked at Gus and asked, "How is it you seem to know exactly what I need, right at the time I need it? Who are you, Gus? And how do you know so much about me?"

"All in good time, pal. Right now, ya have some business inside this store."

Michael shut the back door and moved to the window on the driver's side of the taxi. "You're about as helpful as this Blake fellow, you know that, Gus?"

"Ya got nothin' ta worry about workin' with the captain and me, pal," Gus said, slipping the taxi in gear. "If that pushy sister of yours ever gets wind of what's goin' on here and gets herself involved in yer case, then ya got worries."

"My sister?!" Michael gasped as Gus pulled the taxi away. "What about my sister?" But it was no use. All Michael got for an answer to his question was a look at the back of the taxi as it rounded the corner. Michael shrugged and crossed the street to the store. Walking through the door, he went immediately to the counter. "May I help you?" the young woman asked.

Michael noticed she was wearing a name tag. "Yes, Jennifer," he answered. "I'd like to send an e-mail. Is that one of your services here?"

Jennifer smiled. "You bet," she assured him. "You can send an e-mail anywhere in the world from here. We charge two-fifty for the first one hundred words."

"That's great. Next question, can I receive a fax here?"

"Absolutely," Jennifer assured him.

Michael pulled the drawing he had made at the cafe from his shirt pocket. "I need to have this scanned into the e-mail," he said, handing the picture to Jennifer. "And I'll need a picture of myself, as well as a computer to type out my message. Can you do all that?"

"That's what we're in business for," she smiled. "You can use the computer over there to type your message. In the meantime, I'll set up the camera."

Michael nodded and crossed the room to the computer where he sat down and composed his letter:

Dear Ms. Jenee,

I have a rather large problem that I hope you might be able to help me with. Keeping it to the point, let me just say I'm experiencing a severe memory loss. I happened onto your picture at Miss Alissa's Bookstore here in Miami. I have a strong feeling that we've met at some time. I'm sending a picture of myself in the hope you might recognize me. I'm also sending a second picture I hope you can identify for me. You can fax your reply to the address included with this e-mail. Send it to the attention of Michael Allen. And yes, I am aware that my name is the same as the detective in your book, which is all the more reason why I feel you might know me. I'll check back in a few hours to see if you've had a chance to respond. Thanks for any help you may be able to give me.

Michael

His business finished at Copymasters, Michael stepped outside and checked for any sign of Gus's taxi. No such luck this time. What he did see, however, was a black-and-white patrol car moving slowly down the street, as though the officers inside were looking for something, or someone, in particular. Michael pulled his hat down and looked away until the patrol car disappeared around a corner. Walking at a fast clip in the opposite direction from the one the patrol car had taken, Michael had gone only a couple of blocks when he spotted a sign hanging over the sidewalk advertising rooms for rent. The place wasn't much, but he needed somewhere to stay, at least until he had time to check back on his e-mail. He stepped inside and rented a room.

Flopping down on the bed, he opened Alexis Jenee's novel and began reading. The author told an intriguing story about a diamond thief who outsmarted everyone except her hero named Michael, the detective and main character in her book. The detective managed to stay one step ahead of the thief and eventually cornered him in a deserted warehouse where he was trying to fence the stolen diamonds.

Michael thought it was an interesting coincidence the author had chosen his name for her detective. He could only hope she would respond to his e-mail, and maybe, just maybe could shed some light on the mystery of his life.

Michael tired of reading and lay the book aside to rest his eyes. As he did, he was caught up in another sudden burst of restored memory. He saw himself in a diver's suit, somewhere in ocean waters. Was it the Atlantic? Something from within his foggy mind assured him it was indeed. And he wasn't alone there. There was another swimmer at his side. She was wearing a diver's mask, but he knew her face all the same. It was the face he had drawn at the cafe. He felt an unbelievable attraction to this woman. He suddenly wished he could hold her, kiss her lips, stroke her long blond hair. Who could she be, and why the feeling she somehow desperately needed him right now?

More questions crossed his mind. What had they been doing in the Atlantic Ocean? He sensed they were looking for something. Something important. The image of an old chest came to him. Michael was sure the chest contained whatever it was they were looking for. He relaxed and was just about to drop off to sleep when another scene came to mind. This time he and the woman were aboard a small boat. There were others there with them. Somewhere a gun flashed. There was a burst of pain in Michael's head. The woman screamed out his name. After that, nothing but blackness. He searched for more, but the temporary window into the unknown had closed. There was no more. Not for now, at least.

He glanced at his watch to see that it was nearly noon. A smile crossed his lips as he contemplated the events of his morning. Not a bad day's activity for a man shot in the head. Closing his eyes again, he relaxed. In a moment, he was fast asleep.

* * *

Detective Darwell was just testing the water in his new cooler when the phone rang again. "Darwell here. Talk to me."

"It's Becky at the switchboard, Detective Darwell. You said to notify you if any word came in on the missing John Doe."

"Yeah, Becky, what have you got?"

"Car 74 came in to pick up the picture of the man. They think they saw him earlier. At least the guy looked like him, black hat and all. He was in the neighborhood of Murphy's Pawn Shop, if you know where that is."

Darwell tossed away his paper cup. "What cop doesn't know that neighborhood, Becky? Just the sort of place I'd expect this guy to hide out. I'm sure he has plenty of friends down there. I want every store, every flophouse, every building in the neighborhood checked, ya got that? Tell 'em I said don't let an area the size of a postage stamp go unchecked. We got him boxed in, and I don't want him slipping out. And let me know the instant you hear anything. I'll be on my cell phone. I'm about to pay Murphy a little visit at his pawn shop."

* * *

Michael woke from his dream and struggled to keep it alive just a few seconds longer. He had dreamed he was looking into the face of an angel. Pulling the watch from his pocket, he quickly opened it and stared at the woman's picture there. "It's her," he gasped aloud. "I was dreaming of my sister, Sam." And then it hit him, his sister really was an angel. At first, the thought came with a tinge of sorrow, but as he remembered more about Sam, his feelings grew warm and tender. Yes, she was an angel. A very beautiful and happy angel. But where was she now? How could she have let him be shot? And why wasn't she here helping him remember?

He didn't have the answer but he was getting used to the feeling. "At least I know my own name now," he said aloud. "And I know I have an angel of a sister named Sam."

"Aye, matey, that be the truth. Ye do have a sister named Sam. And she be an angel, says I."

"Captain Blake! You're back again." Then another light suddenly turned on. "It's true!" Michael exclaimed. "My sister Sam *is* an angel! And so are you! That's how you've done all those remarkable things."

"Aye, that I be. And ye be warmin' me heart with your rememberin'. But right now I has a warnin' for ye, laddie. Yer quarters are about to be invaded, says I. It be time to desert the ship. Out the window with ye, lad. And be quick about it."

Any thoughts of protest Michael might have had were quickly erased when he heard heavy footsteps on the stairs leading to the second floor of the apartment house where his room was situated. In a flash, he was out of the bed and scrambling through the already open window.

CHAPTER 11

"All right, Maggie, I want to know what's going on here, and I want to know right now!"

Maggie's heart sank. She had been so involved with the contract on her computer screen that she'd failed to hear Samantha and Jason approach her desk. "Sam!" she gasped. "What are you doing here? How did you get here?"

"What I'm doing here is trying to find out why my intuition is tearing me apart. How I got here is a good question, indeed. Especially since *someone* left specific instructions there would be no early transportation available to Jason and me. Why would that *someone* do that, Maggie?"

Maggie stood to face her unexpected guests. "I'm sure you know whose idea it was to block your transportation, Sam. And I'm sure if you think about it, you'll know it was for your own good. You and Jason deserved the vacation we planned for you." Maggie released a dejected sigh. "But you couldn't leave well enough alone, could you?"

Samantha shook her head. "Something is wrong here, Maggie. I just know it. And it concerns my brother, doesn't it?"

Maggie reached over and hit the save command on her computer. "I have to know, Sam. How did you manage it? I know you couldn't have convinced the travel agency to bring you home, not after the fear I put in them."

"You want to know how I got home? I'll tell you how I got home—just as soon as you tell me what's going on with my brother, Maggie." Samantha gave Maggie a warning look. "And don't try to whitewash it, either. I know something's wrong."

Maggie laughed. "I should have known I couldn't keep you away, Sam. You're right; there are a few problems. Nothing big enough that Gus and I can't handle," she quickly pointed out. "Gus and I are both on the job." Maggie paused, drew a breath, then amended her statement. "At least we're both on the job now, that is."

"Oh no," Samantha groaned. "Are you telling me there was a time when Gus was left alone on the job?"

"Yes," Maggie sighed.

"What did he do, Maggie? Is my brother in trouble?"

Maggie's eyes shifted from Samantha to Jason then back to Samantha. "Maybe the two of you should sit down," she suggested, "while I fill you in."

* * *

Detective Darwell was first to reach the apartment door. Grabbing the knob, he found it locked. Hurling his shoulder against the door, he struggled to force it open. It didn't budge. Again he slammed his weight into the door with the same results. Turning to face the gaping faces of the officers behind him, he threw up both hands and shouted. "Get me a key! Why is it they always put dead bolts on these flophouse doors? Get me a key, now!"

The excited apartment manager wriggled his way through the officers and tried to insert the key into the lock. Darwell grabbed it from his hand and did the honors himself. Pushing the door open, he rushed into the room, gun drawn, and made a quick evaluation. One look inside the bathroom, and he kicked the wall in anger. Then he spotted the window. In an instant he was to it, looking down at the figure just stepping off the retractable ladder of the fire escape.

"YOU!" he shouted. "HOLD IT RIGHT THERE!"

Michael paid him no heed but darted for the far end of the alley in the opposite direction of where he could see the squad cars parked.

"What is it with bad guys these days?" Darwell growled as he squeezed through the window onto the fire escape ledge. "They're all hard of hearing. I distinctly told that guy to hold it."

"I can get off a shot!" one of the officers behind Darwell who was holding a rifle cried out. "You want me to bring him down, Detective?"

"No, I don't want you to shoot him!" Darwell exclaimed while stepping onto the retractable ladder that had automatically retracted when Michael's weight no longer held it down. "This guy is going to lead me to the others! I want him alive!"

Darwell hit the ground just as Michael was rounding the corner at the end of the alley. In one split second, Darwell was after him on a dead run. Once he reached the end of the alley himself, Darwell stared at the empty street where Michael had disappeared. Nothing but shops on either side of the street, and no sign at all of the man he was after. Grabbing his two-way radio, he barked into it. "We got a rat in a hole here somewhere, boys. I want this whole area cordoned off. Don't let so much as a cockroach out of here."

Holding his pistol waist high, Darwell started walking slowly down the street in the direction he had seen Michael go. The first door he came to opened into a secondhand clothing store. There were no customers; only a single clerk stood next to the counter. "You, slick," Darwell called out, flashing his badge from inside the flap of his overcoat. "Did you see a guy run past here?"

"Yeah," the clerk said. "I saw a guy. Running like a whirlwind was chasin' him, ya might say."

"This way?" Darwell asked, pointing down the street.

"Ya got it, pal," the clerk confirmed. "That's the way he was headed."

Darwell glanced ahead along the street just in time to see a patrol car pull out from a side street at the far end of the block. "We got him now," he muttered to himself. "One rat about to snap the jaws of the trap."

Within seconds the police officers came out of the woodwork. They were everywhere, checking every store on the block. Both sides of the street. Suddenly, a movement above him caught Darwell's eye. Someone was on the roof of the building he was standing in front of. "He's on the roof!" Darwell shouted. "How in the name of Paul Bunyan's ox did he get on the roof? This guy must shower with Vaseline soap."

* * *

As Michael rounded the building leading from the alley to the street, he spotted Captain Blake standing in front of a secondhand clothing store. "This way, matey—through here, says I." Blake pointed inside the store.

Michael didn't hesitate. He darted inside where he spotted, of all people, Gus behind the counter. "Gus," he gasped. "First you're a cook, then a cabbie, now you're a used-clothes salesman?"

"What can I say, pal? I'm whatever I need to be at the moment. Through the door at the back. Get up the stairs and onto the roof. Captain Blake will take it from there."

Michael made the back door in three bounds. By the time he reached the top of the stairs, his head was throbbing. This was not the sort of thing for a man with a gunshot wound to the head to be doing.

"This way, matey," Blake called, pointing to a wooden ladder that led to an opening into the attic. Michael paused only a second or two at the bottom of the ladder to catch his breath, then he was up it. Pushing the board used to cover the opening out of the way, he climbed into the attic. It was dark, but he could see light at one end coming through a louvered vent. Very carefully, he made his way to the vent, where he determined that it did, in fact, lead to the roof. He remove the louvered guard and squeezed through the opening. That's when he made the mistake of moving too close to the edge of the roof. Darwell spotted him before he could scamper back far enough to be out of sight.

"What do I do now, Blake?" he called out, ducking as low as possible.

"This way, me friend," Blake called from the far side of the roof. "Ye be about ready to play trapeze artist, says I."

"Trapeze artist?" Michael asked, moving quickly to Blake's side. "Please tell me you don't expect me to jump to the next building."

'No, matey, I be not expectin' that of ye. However, I will be askin' ye to walk the plank off this building."

"What?! You mean like jump?"

"Aye, that be me meanin'. Me friend, Gus will be breakin' yer fall."

Michael realized he was on the alley side of the building now. The same alley he had ran down only minutes earlier. He moved to the side of the building and glanced down. There was a truck there. A big one, with an open bed. And of all things, the bed was filled with what appeared to be secondhand clothes. "You expect me to jump into that truck?" he blurted out.

"That, or me friend Gus will push ye, says I. Either way, it be your means of escape, me lad."

Michael looked at the truck again. "You're sure about this?" he pressed.

"I be sure, matey. Just take the first step. I'll be right beside ye."

"Yeah, but you're already dead, Blake!"

Michael could see there was little use in arguing further. Drawing in a breath, he jumped. To his relief, the soft clothing broke the fall. He quickly buried himself under the garments.

* * *

"Find a way to get on that roof!" Darwell shouted. "And beef up the security in the area. This guy is like a cat. I don't want him slipping out of my grasp again!"

Sirens were screaming in every direction from where Darwell stood pacing back and forth in front of the clothing store. Suddenly, a truck emerged from the alley behind him. "Hold it right there!" he shouted at the driver. In two steps he was on the running board of the truck, his pistol pointed at the nose of the driver. "Where do you think you're going, slick? We have a situation here, and no one is moving in or out until I give the okay."

Darwell looked suspiciously at the load of clothing through the guard rails of the open bed truck, then back to the driver. His eyes stopped. "You're the fellow who was just inside the store there, aren't you, slick?" he asked.

"Yer pretty observant, pal," Gus answered. "I'd like to stay and chat, but I got things ta do. Ya mind movin' back a step so I can be on my way."

Darwell slammed his hand down on the top of the truck cab. "You ain't goin' nowhere, slick. You don't know who you're talking to, do you? The name's Curtis Darwell. Detective Curtis Darwell to you. Now get out of that cab so I can have a closer look at this load."

Gus smiled. "Maybe you oughta let me introduce myself, pal. Name's Gus. Special Conditions Coordinator, Second Level—Gus, to you. Now let me ask ya this, Detective What's-yer-name. Do ya always walk around pointin' plastic squirt guns in yer suspects' faces?"

"What is this?" Darwell shouted. "We have a comedian! Right in the middle of a police situation, we find ourselves a comedian. Does this look like a squirt gun to you, slick?" Darwell shoved the pistol right up to Gus' nose.

"Looks plastic to me, pal. One just like ya can buy in any K-Mart store anywhere in the universe."

Darwell glanced nonchalantly at the gun. One look and his attitude of indifference changed to one of complete and absolute confusion. He *was* holding a squirt gun. But how? And who—? In the middle of his dilemma, he suddenly felt himself being hurled away from the truck—as if by some invisible hand. He struck the pavement with a stunning thud. Quickly gathering his wits, he shot to his feet in time to see the truck passing the positioned squad cars without the slightest hint of opposition. All his fellow officers were standing there, doing absolutely nothing to intercept the truck. They all looked like their feet were glued to the pavement.

"Stop that truck!" Darwell loudly demanded.

Someone tried to start the engine of a squad car, but it only ground uselessly until the battery ran dead. Just like that, the truck was gone. And with it, the suspect. There was no doubt in Darwell's mind of that.

Darwell held up the squirt gun where he could get a good look at it. "Heads are going to roll," he grumbled under his breath. "When I catch the guy who switched this gun . . ."

He looked again at the scene surrounding him. The officers had come alive again now that the suspect was out of the trap. Darwell just shook his head. Then, walking over to the closest squad car, he leaned in the window and addressed the officer at the wheel. "Get on the horn, slick. I want to know who this Gus character is that was driving that truck. And I want to know what a Special Conditions Coordinator, Second Level, is while we're about it!"

"Yes, sir," the officer said, grabbing his mike. "I'm on it."

Darwell spun away from the car, then in utter disgust he headed back to the room where his slippery suspect had been holed up. On the bed, he found two items. There was a black Stetson hat and a novel. "Well what do you know?" Darwell said. "Our boy likes mystery novels." Removing his cell phone, he dialed the number for Becky at the switchboard. "Becky," he said, once she was on the line. "Darwell here. I need you to check something out for me. See what you can dig up on an author who goes by the name of Alexis Jenee. And check on her book, *The Man Who Loved Diamonds*. I want to know every bookstore in this city that sells the book."

"Consider it done," Becky answered. "And we had a streak of good luck in this case, Detective. We located the owners of the boat your mystery man had rented, and they were able to ID him. His name's Michael Allen; he's a freelance artist. We ran a check on him and he's as clean as this week's laundry."

"The guy's clean? That don't add up. He must be good at covering his tracks, I'd say."

"Maybe not," Becky proposed. "Maybe the stuff you found on him was a plant. It has been known to happen."

"Not this time," Darwell shot back. "I have a feeling about this one. He's guilty all right. And—he's going to lead me to rest of his gang of bad guys. They've eluded me far too long now. Their luck is about to run dry. Count on it, Becky. And good work."

* * *

Michael sensed the truck pull to a stop. He listened for voices, but all he could hear was the sound of his own breathing. Very cautiously, he moved some of the clothing aside and peered out through the slats in the truck bed. He checked one way and then the other to find the street clear in both directions. He sat up and checked the truck cab. Gus was gone. No surprises here. Nor was he surprised to discover the truck was parked across the street from Copymasters. It was becoming more and more obvious he wasn't alone in his plight; without question, there were angels on duty. And it was obvious that this Gus character was a senior angel to Captain Blake. Blake had even called Gus "a second-level angel." Where had Michael heard that term before?

"That's it!" he cried out. "I remember! Sam talked about being a second-level angel!" Michael had only been allowed to see Sam once since she crossed the line to become an angel. But she had told him several things when he did see her. Now he understood. Gus was a second-level angel, while the captain was a first level. "I'm a lucky man to have these guys in my corner right now," he confessed to himself. With this confession came a new confidence that he would soon remember everything.

He glanced across the street to Copymasters. If Gus had brought him here, it probably meant there was something waiting for him inside. Suddenly, Michael remembered his hat. Of all the stupid things to do. In his haste to leave the room when Detective Darwell showed up, he had forgotten the hat. This was not good, especially with Darwell hot on his heels. The bandaged head would make him too darned conspicuous. No doubt about it, he needed a hat. But wait—he was standing in a truckload of discarded clothing. He began rummaging through the piles of clothing. He pulled out a ball cap. "Dallas Cowboys?" he grimaced. "Of all the teams in all the sports—I had to come up with a Dallas Cowboys hat. I hate the Dallas Cowboys. Ah, what the heck, beggars can't be choosers." He put on the hat and climbed down from the truck. Crossing the street, he entered the store and approached the counter.

To his pleasant surprise, he was again greeted by Jennifer, the same young woman who had waited on him earlier. Jennifer smiled at seeing him. "Good," she said. "I was hoping you would show up." She picked up an envelope from the basket on the counter and handed it to him. "This fax came in not half an hour ago."

"Thank you," Michael said, as he took the envelope from her. He was just about to open it, when he glanced across the street where the truck was parked. A surge of fright passed through him like a bolt of lightning from the sky. Two black-and-white patrol cars had just pulled up and had the truck pinned in from both sides. The door to one patrol car opened and two officers stepped out, guns drawn. Very cautiously, they approached the truck.

Michael glanced at Jennifer. Her attention was glued to the commotion across the street. He had to think of something and he had to do it fast. He figured there was a back door to this place, but he had to find a way of getting out it without arousing Jennifer's suspicion. Spotting an X-Acto knife on the counter, Michael grabbed a couple of tissues from the tissue box on the counter. Next, he turned as if to leave, allowing the back of his hand to brush against the razor sharp blade of the X-Acto knife. "Ouch!" he cried, raising his hand high enough for her to see small drops of blood oozing from the wound. "How clumsy of me. Do you have a restroom where I can wash this off?"

Jennifer quickly picked up the X-Acto knife and slid its protective cover in place. The look on her face assured Michael of her concern. "Uh, yes," she was quick to respond. "Through that door to the back room. We normally don't allow our customers to use the facilities, but—"

"I understand," Michael assured her, already halfway to the door she had pointed to. "If I can just wash this off, it'll be fine."

Jennifer stared after him, never moving from where she stood. Once in the back room, Michael spotted a door he guessed would lead outside. He pushed it open and stepped into the alley. Blotting away the small amount of blood on his hand with the tissue taken from the counter, he walked briskly away. Exiting the alley at the far end, he turned onto the street and continued walking for several blocks. At last, he ducked into a laundromat and moved to the back of the room. After assuring himself there were no customers in the place, he pulled out the fax and read it.

Michael, of course I know you. I never told you this, but I borrowed your name for the detective in my latest novel.

"Hmm," Michael said. "She did pattern her hero after me. I wonder how that happened." He read on.

I also recognized the picture of Jenice.

"Jenice," Michael repeated aloud. "Is that her name? I just can't remember." Again, he turned back to the message.

We only met once, and that was on a tiny island in the Caribbean Sea. I lived there at the time with my brother, Brad, and my daughter, Tanielle. You and Jenice landed on the island quite unexpectedly, but that's a long story. If you don't recall it, I'll gladly refresh your memory when we meet. I just happen to be in Miami at the moment. My publisher is based in Miami and I'm here promoting my newly released novel. Give me a call as soon as you receive this message. The phone number of my hotel suite is 555-7070. I'm in room 875. I know I can help you. And, by the way, my real name is Shannon Douglas. Alexis Jenee is simply a pen name.

Michael reread the note three times. Then, glancing around, he saw a pay phone on the back wall of the laundromat. Rushing to the phone, he deposited two coins and dialed the number she had given him.

"Hello?"

"Uh, hello. Is this Shannon Douglas?"

"Yes, this is Shannon. Are you by chance Michael Allen?"

"I think that's who I am," he stammered. "About now, I'm not sure about much of anything."

"Then it's true. You have lost your memory."

"I have a head wound," he explained. "I don't know when it happened but I woke up in the hospital yesterday. I've recovered a few things, but I'm a long way from home, I'm afraid."

"Okay," she said. "I can help. We need to meet somewhere. Do you have transportation?"

Michael admitted he did not.

"All right. Do you have any idea where you are then?"

"At the moment I'm in a laundromat. I doubt that's much help, but how about a place called Miss Alissa's Books? Does that ring any bells?"

"I know exactly where Miss Alissa's bookshop is located. I've done several book signings there. I could be there in half an hour. Will that work for you?"

Michael seriously considered whether he should confide his problem with Detective Darwell or not. The way he saw it, he had little choice but to confide in Shannon. "I, uh, may have one problem meeting you at the bookstore," he responded soberly. "I have no idea how it happened, but my memory loss is the result of a gunshot wound to my head."

"A gunshot wound?! That sounds serious, Michael."

"It gets worse. Whoever did this must have planted drugs on me. So the police have me on their 'most wanted' list at the moment. So far I've been able to stay one step ahead of them, but . . ."

"You were shot, someone planted drugs, and now the police are looking for you? Be honest with me, Michael. Are you innocent?"

"Like I told you, Shannon. I have no memory of who I am or how I fit into society. But this much I do know, I'm not a drug dealer. If I'd ever had a run-in with the law, I'd know about it. I'm sure I'd know."

"That's good enough for me, Michael. I write detective stories, remember? Who knows what material I might glean from helping you out. I'll be at Miss Alissa's Bookstore in half an hour. I'll have a friend with me. His name is Tom, and you can trust him. We'll be in a rental car, a white Toyota Camry."

"All right, I'll do my best to meet you at the bookstore. But if the police are patrolling . . ."

"If the police are there, we'll just have to cross that bridge when we come to it. Just keep an eye out for a white Toyota with me inside. You've seen my picture, so you should have no trouble recognizing me."

"I'll be watching, Shannon. And—thanks."

Michael hung up the phone and moved to the front door of the laundromat. A quick check outside revealed the street to be clear of any patrol cars. He wasn't exactly sure where the laundromat was with respect to the bookstore, but he figured it would be two to three blocks at the most. Pulling his cap down tight, he stepped onto the street and began walking, keeping as close to the buildings as possible. If he happened to see a black and white, he could dart inside one of the stores that lined the sidewalk. At last, he rounded a corner and spotted the bookstore half a block away. Pulling out his watch, he marked the time. It was still at least twenty minutes before Shannon would be at the store. Then he remembered the cafe across the street from the bookstore. That might be a good place to wait. He wondered if Gus would be there this time.

Michael moved swiftly down the street and entered the cafe. No Gus. And this time there were other customers. Several of them. There was still only one waitress, a real one this time.

Selecting a booth near the front window, Michael took a seat and opened the menu. He ordered a burger, fries, and a soft drink. He barely had time to finish his food when the Toyota pulled up in front of the bookstore.

Michael dropped a ten-dollar bill on the table and hurried outside. He didn't recognize the male driver, but he could see Shannon beside him in the front seat. By the time he reached the car, Shannon had already seen him. "Hurry," she said, through the open car window. "Jump in the back."

Michael opened the door and got in quickly. "Duck your head down," Shannon directed. "Just in case some of your badge-carrying friends happen by."

Michael had barely closed his door when a woman rushed unexpectedly from inside the bookstore and came up to the car window. "Shannon?" she exclaimed excitedly. "I saw you from inside. Are you here to sign books?"

"Oh, uh, hi, Miss Alissa," Shannon responded nervously. "Actually, no. I had planned on signing a few, but I just received an emergency call on my cell phone. Something has come up that I must see to immediately. You will forgive me if I beg off this time, won't you, Miss Alissa?"

Miss Alissa glanced at the back seat where Michael was doing his best to pull the ball cap over his face. "I hope it isn't anything too serious," she muttered.

"Oh no. Nothing too serious," Shannon assured her. "But it's something that does need my attention without delay. I'll give you a call before coming next time, okay?"

"Sure, that will be fine," Miss Alissa nodded her head, her eyes darting back and forth between Shannon in the front seat and Michael in the back. "With a little advance notice, I'll have a chance to advertise your visit to the store. Very good for business, you know."

"I'll call," Shannon assured her, at the same time nudging Tom with her left elbow. He took the hint and eased the car forward. Once Miss Alissa was clear, he floored the accelerator and sped away.

* * *

Miss Alissa stared dumbfounded at the departing Toyota and wondered why Shannon had acted so strangely. It definitely wasn't like her. She was about to shrug it off and return to the store when her attention was drawn to an approaching patrol car that slowed and pulled up alongside her. The plainclothes officer inside flashed a badge and shot out a question, "Excuse me, Miss. May I assume from the t-shirt that you work at this bookstore?"

"Actually, I'm the owner," she responded. "I wear the same t-shirt that all my employees do. Advertising—great for business, you know."

Darwell handed her Michael's picture. "Ever see this cowboy?" he asked. "I have reason to believe he may have been in your store earlier today."

Miss Alissa looked closely at the picture. A cold shiver ran up her spine as she recognized the man. "Yes," she responded. "I've seen him twice. He was in my store this morning. He bought a copy of *The Man Who Loved Diamonds.*"

"I'm familiar with the book, ma'am." Darwell flashed the copy he had taken from Michael's room earlier. "You said you'd seen this guy twice. When was the second time?"

Miss Alissa's eyes lit up when she saw the book. "Good choice of reading material, officer. A detective book, a real thriller. I'm betting you can't put it down until it's finished."

Darwell pointed a finger at the picture she was holding. "The second time you saw this guy—I'd really like to hear about it if it's not too much trouble."

Miss Alissa glared at him. "No sense in getting in a dither over the matter," she said. "If you really want to talk with this man, he's probably less than two blocks from here right now. He was in that white Toyota that pulled away just as you came up."

Darwell slammed the dashboard with a clenched fist. He turned to the officer at the wheel. "Get on the radio, slick! We have a white Toyota Camry loose in the neighborhood. I want it found, and I want it stopped. Is that asking too much?"

Darwell faced Miss Alissa again. "There were more people in the car. Who were they?"

"If you'll look on the back page of that book you threw to the seat," Miss Alissa said primly, "you'll see the picture of one of them."

He grabbed the book. "The woman who wrote this book is in the car with our cowboy? Alexis—what's her name?"

"Her name is Shannon Douglas," Miss Alissa informed him. "Alexis Jenee is her pen name."

In an instant, Darwell had his cell phone out and was punching in numbers. "Becky," he said, as soon as she answered. "Take down this name. Shannon Douglas. I want to know everything there is to know about her. She has something to hide, I'd stake my life on it. She writes books under a fake name. No one uses a fake name unless they have something to hide."

"The pen name," Becky responded. "I may need it if you want all I can dig up on this lady."

Darwell covered the mouthpiece. "Alexis what?" he asked the store owner.

"Alexis Jenee. She spells it J-e-n-e-e."

"Alexis Jenee, Becky," Darwell said back into the phone. "That's spelled J-e-n-e-e."

"I'm on it, Detective. So how's the chase coming with this Michael person?"

"I got him, Becky. I'm fixing to close the trap. Gotta go, lady. Keep me posted." He shoved the cell phone back in his coat pocket and looked back at the store owner. "There was another man in the Toyota. Can you make him?"

Miss Alissa looked startled, then her face cleared. "Can I identify him, is that what you mean?"

"Right, lady, can you *identify* the man?" Darwell came back with a look of disgust.

"I only know him as Tom," she explained. "He and Shannon are—well—you know. Shannon told me once that he was the man she should have married."

Darwell pulled out his notebook and jotted down a few notes. "You've been a great help, miss," he said, never looking up from his notes. "Keep up the good work. We need more concerned citizens like you." He closed the notebook and glanced over at the driver. "We gonna sit here all day, slick? What do you say we find ourselves a white Toyota?"

CHAPTER 12

Gus's timing couldn't have been more appropriate—or, inappropriate if you will—depending on whose point of view it was. He entered the office just as Maggie was finishing her explanation to Samantha and Jason. Samantha immediately turned on him, her eyes ablaze with displeasure. Gus stopped dead in his tracks, a horrified look filling his face. "Now hold on, Sam," he said in hurried self-defense. "Before ya say a word, let me assure ya that Michael is perfectly all right. I have everything under control."

In one bound Samantha was in front of him, an angry finger waving in his face. "You got my brother shot, Gus! You let the bad guys frame him with drugs! You left him wide open to the relentless pursuit of this Darwell character who seems to think he's Wyatt Earp! And you even managed to let Jenice get kidnapped! You call that having everything under control?"

Gus shrugged. "So I had a couple of insignificant little setbacks. Cut me some slack, Sam. Everythin's rollin' along smooth as grass at the moment."

"That's 'smooth as glass,' Gus," Samantha said. Then, lowering her finger, she released a long sigh. Looking him in the eye, she said, "I have to hand it to you for the way you handled that pushy detective. You did good."

But just as Gus was about to relax, Samantha raised her finger again. "But not good enough, Gus! I'm sorry, but I just can't trust you to finish this project, not since it involves Michael and Jenice. You know darn well this project should have been mine and Jason's right up front."

Gus grinned, and let his shoulders rise in another shrug. "Hey, Sam, if ya want me ta step aside, all ya gotta do is ask."

Samantha's hand dropped and her expression softened. "I want you to step aside, Gus. I realize you and Maggie have the authority to overrule me if you chose, but I'd really like to handle this one myself."

Gus glanced over at Maggie who gave him a thumbs-up. "If yer sure that's what ya want, Sam, who am I ta stand in yer way? But I just hafta ask. How in blue blazes did ya get here from yer vacation when Maggie had it all figured to keep ya out there?"

"Yes," Maggie added with a smile of her own. "I'd like to hear the answer to that one myself."

Samantha grinned. "Ask this cute little husband of mine," she said. "And you might be surprised at the answer he'll cook up."

* * *

"This is my friend, Tom Reddings," Shannon told Michael, as they sped away.

"Glad to meet you, Tom," Michael said. "I really appreciate what the two of you are doing to help me."

Shannon turned to look at Michael. "How bad is your memory loss?" she asked. "Do you have any memory at all?"

"Some," he acknowledged. "I at least know my name now. I know I have a sister Sam, who's—well, I like to call her an angel. I have a slight memory of being shot, and I have this feeling about the lady in the picture I sent you. You called her Jenice. I'm sure she plays a big part in my life, but it's more a feeling than a memory." He looked up until their eyes met. "What else can you tell me about myself?"

"You and I met only once," Shannon answered thoughtfully. "On the island, as I mentioned in my fax."

"Jenice," Michael echoed, trying desperately to remember. "Does she have a last name?"

Shannon nodded. "Anderson," she said. "Jenice Anderson."

Hearing Jenice's full name came to Michael like a ray of morning sunlight penetrating the blackness of a predawn sky. "I remember!" he exclaimed. "Jenice and I are to be married! No wonder I couldn't get her picture out of my mind. We're supposed to be married next month, Shannon!"

Michael rubbed his forehead with the tip of his middle finger. "And I remember you, Shannon! I remember that morning on the island, you were writing a novel."

"Yes!" she exclaimed. "The one I just had published. With Michael Allen as my go-get-'em detective. Like I told you before, I stole your name for my hero."

A look of horror suddenly filled Michael's eyes. "Jenice is in danger!" he shouted. "The men who shot me—they've taken her captive."

"What?!" Tom broke in. "Do you have any idea where they've taken her?"

Michael rubbed his head again, being careful not to disturb the bandage. "It's coming back," he groaned. "Jenice and I were on a boat somewhere between the Atlantic Ocean and the Caribbean Sea. I was shot, and the next thing I remember is someone trying to wake me. It must have been the Coast Guard when they found me in the boat. I vaguely remember being tied in a metal basket and hoisted up to a helicopter by a steel cable. After that, there's nothing until I woke up in the hospital. They've taken Jenice. I know they've taken her, but I have no idea where."

"I know where she be, matey," Blake said. For the first time, Michael noticed the captain sitting in the seat next to him. "She be on me island," Blake continued. "The very island ye be rememberin' just now."

Michael looked back and forth between Blake and those in the front seat. He understood very little about dealing with angels, or ghosts if you will. But this much he did understand. Neither Tom nor Shannon were aware of Captain Blake's presence. They couldn't see him, and they couldn't hear him. But Blake had just told him where Jenice could be found. His mind raced. He needed these people's help, but how could he explain the presence of an angel? And if he didn't explain the angel, how could he explain his suddenly knowing where Jenice was? He bit his lip and decided to go for it. He blurted it out. "I know where she is! She's on the Caribbean island where you and Brad once lived, Shannon."

Shannon looked surprised. "How can you be so certain, Michael?" she asked. "You just said you didn't know for sure where she was?"

"I—uh—it's hard to explain. It's like a voice just told me, but I'm sure that's where she is. On the island."

Shannon glanced over her shoulder at Michael. There was a long moment of silence, followed by a question. "A voice told you she's on the island? What sort of a voice?"

"Well, I, it's really hard to explain, Shannon."

What Shannon said next came like a bombshell to Michael. "Could this voice you heard possibly have anything to do with a sea captain by the name of Horatio Symington Blake?"

Michael's face showed his astonishment. "You know about the captain?" he gasped.

"I've never met the captain personally," Shannon explained, "but my brother, Brad, was on a first-name basis with him for the ten years we lived on the island. Brad tried to hide the captain from Tanielle and me, but we were onto him. It got to the point where I could feel the captain's presence whenever he came around. I feel him right now, Michael. He's in the back seat with you, isn't he? You can see and talk with him exactly as my brother did, can't you?"

Michael was amazed. He wanted to tell her the truth, but he wasn't certain how Tom would take the news. It was Tom himself who set Michael's mind at ease. Glancing in the rearview mirror, he said, "Don't worry about me, Michael. Shannon's told me all about the ghost of Captain Blake. She's explained what a decent sort of fellow the captain must be. I know she wouldn't lie. Tell the captain hello for me and ask him if he's positive Jenice is on the island."

Captain Blake smiled. "I be positive, matey," he responded.

"The captain says he's positive," Michael passed along numbly.

Shannon became serious. "If Captain Blake says Jenice is on the island, then you can bet that's exactly where she is. If there's one thing I know about Captain Blake, it's that his word is his bond."

"The lassie be speaking the truth, matey. And now that yer memory is out of drydock, I can be telling ye what needs to be done. Ye need to be getting yerself out to that island, says I."

"Blake says I need to get to that island," Michael said. "Jenice needs me. But how am I supposed to get there when the police are everywhere looking for me?"

Tom turned the Toyota into a Wal-Mart parking lot and stopped near the back of the lot. He picked a spot an aisle or two away from any other cars. "I know how to get you to the island," he said, pulling out his cell phone. "I'm an air force pilot, Michael. One phone call to a close friend at MacDill Air Force Base in Tampa Bay, and your air taxi will be on the way."

* * *

Stuart Fox's twin outboard boat sped at high speed toward the small island. He and Max Yorty were the only two on board. "I'm fairly familiar with some of the small islands in these parts, Max," Stuart said, shouting to be heard over the noise of the engines. "This one's a virtual jungle. Unless we get a break, we could end up playing cat and mouse with these two from now until your pal Lefty turns opera singer. I got an idea, though. I looked the island over from the telescope on the top deck of the yacht. There's one huge chunk of volcanic rock on the east side that towers over the rest of the island. I plan on putting in as close as possible to the peak. If we get lucky, we just might be able to spot something from the top of it."

"Sure, boss. Sounds like a plan to me. I want that broad, and I want her bad."

Stuart laughed. "You better watch out with that one, Max. She's already won the first couple of rounds. I suggest whatever you have in mind for her be done from a healthy distance. She's a tiger if ever I saw one."

Now it was Max's turn to laugh. "Taming tigers can fun sometimes, boss. I think I might just take my own sweet time taming this one."

Stuart swung the boat to the right, putting him on a course for the east shore. "Yeah, well before you start planning your strategy for big cat training, how about digging out a couple of pairs of binoculars from below deck? Then you can get back up here and help me find a suitable place to put this boat ashore."

* * *

Michael's heart was in his throat as he watched the scene unfolding in front of him. From every direction they came. Black-

and-white patrol cars, moving to positions several yards away from
the Toyota, but surrounding it completely. "Oops," Michael said.
"Looks like I've managed to get the two of you in a bit of a jam,
here."

"Don't worry about it," Shannon assured him. "The more material I get for my next book, the better. I've been in jams before. I was
married to James Baxter, in case you've forgotten."

Tom spoke up. "I don't know why Shannon's convinced you're
innocent and need our help, Michael. But since she is, that's all the
assurance I need. If we can stall another five minutes, or so, our taxi
will be here. Any ideas on how to stall them?"

Michael shrugged. "You're the writer, Shannon. What would your
Michael Allen do at a time like this?"

"My advice is ask Captain Blake," she responded. "We can use
some angelic help about now."

"Not to worry, matey," the captain smiled. "Everything be ship-
shape. The winds be at yer back, and yer sails be filled. Trust me, says I."

* * *

Darwell grabbed his bullhorn and stepped from the car. Then,
remembering he had no gun, he turned back to the officer at the wheel.
"Loan me your gun, slick. I seem to have misplaced mine. And don't ask."

The officer removed his revolver and handed it to Darwell.
Darwell then put the bullhorn to his mouth and pressed the button.
"You—in the Toyota. Hold it right where you are. No one's gonna get
hurt here. Just don't do anything stupid. Step out of the car, and place
your hands on top of your head, where I can see them."

Very slowly, the two front doors and one rear door opened. One
by one, they complied with Darwell's demand. "Now that's what I
call smart," Darwell barked. "You folks have a good chance of living
to be very old people."

Darwell shut off the bullhorn. "Keep everyone else back." he
instructed the officer with him. "I want this guy in my own personal
cuffs."

"I don't mean to disagree with you, Detective," the officer
ventured, "but don't you think it would be wiser to wait for the

SWAT team? Those guys are trained to handle situations like this."

"No! Too many people make too many targets! I'll handle this myself. Keep them all back, got it?"

"Yes, sir. Whatever you say."

Darwell raised the bullhorn again. "Okay, I'm coming in. The three of you just pretend you're wax dummies and hold the pose. Ya got that?" He inched forward toward the three. About halfway there, his attention was suddenly drawn to an approaching helicopter. Seeing the military insignia, he turned the bullhorn back to his own officers. "What's that thing doing in my territory?" he shouted. "Get someone on the phone and get that thing out of here!"

Darwell was flabbergasted. The chopper came in until it was hovering directly overhead, and then—of all things—it touched down between him and the Toyota. Right before his bewildered eyes the three scurried to the chopper and began climbing aboard. "I don't believe this!" he bellowed. "This guy is harder to grab than a bar of wet soap. Now he has the United States Air Force bailing him out." He threw up his hands, the bullhorn in one and the borrowed revolver in the other. "My tax dollars are going to support the very guys I'm paid to bring down. Somebody's gonna hear about this, you can bet on it."

Darwell broke into a run. He reached the chopper just as Michael was struggling to get onboard. The others were already inside. Darwell tossed the bullhorn through the open door, then grabbed onto the door to keep it from closing.

* * *

Michael tried to slam the door closed before Darwell reached the chopper. He didn't make it. Darwell pointed his pistol directly at the pilot and shouted, "Shut this carriage down, slick! You're in big trouble, boy! Big trouble! You're gonna wish you'd never learned to fly one of these gadgets by the time I'm finished with you!"

Darwell's words came to Michael's ears with stinging force. Had his efforts to elude this man's bulldog pursuit come down to this? To be taken at gunpoint to some isolated jail cell where all thoughts of going to Jenice's aid would be futile? Michael had had very little time to think about Jenice's situation since recovering his memory. Now it all came crushing down on him like a ton of riverbed rock. Michael had no doubt what the men who held Jenice captive were capable of. He shuddered to think what they must already have put her through. And what must she think of him? She watched them shoot him down in cold blood. How could she possibly suppose he had survived?

But one haunting thought suppressed all else in his mind: would he ever see Jenice alive again? Michael stared at the huge revolver in Darwell's hand, and his heart sank.

CHAPTER 13

Jenice and Roy soon learned that moving through the dense rain-forest without the benefit of knowing the established trails was no cakewalk. After some distance, Roy suggested they take a breather. He sat down on a flat rock and watched Jenice as she chose a fallen log to sit on. He couldn't help but marvel at how beautiful she was. Roy had been in love with Jenice for years. He'd done everything in his power to win her love, but it just never seemed to work out. He could never understand why. He and Jenice were perfectly suited for each other. They were both aggressive reporters, and both loved adventure. For a time, Roy thought he had finally won the battle. Jenice accepted his ring and they even discussed a marriage date. That was the happiest time of Roy's life. Then this Michael Allen stepped in and spoiled everything. What right did Michael have taking Jenice away from him? Roy and Jenice were a team long before Michael came along. It just wasn't fair.

There was no denying it, Roy was ashamed of what he was doing here. Never would he have supposed he could stoop this low. But this was more than just a fight, this was an all-out war. And Jenice Anderson was the prize.

Roy had never intended for Michael to be hurt. He had empha-sized that to Stuart Fox. Roy wondered now how he could ever have been such a fool as to trust the likes of a man like Stuart Fox not to use violence. He could only hope that Michael was alive and that someone had found him in time to get him the help he needed.

The gold meant nothing to Roy. And he had never intended for Stuart and his gang to have it, either. Roy knew Jenice well enough to be sure that she would never reveal the whereabouts of the map. His plan had been to get Jenice to the yacht, away from Michael, and smack in the middle of an adventure as intriguing as Roy could devise. He and Jenice had come through other adventures together as reporters, and it had always been great fun for them both. He thought if he could create one more such adventure for the two of them to share, it just might be enough to wake Jenice up to the fact that the two of them were meant for each other. Michael Allen was an artist, for pity's sake. There was no way a woman like Jenice Anderson could ever be happy with an artist. Roy acknowledged that not only did he want Jenice for himself, he also had a responsibility to keep Jenice from ruining her life with this bogus marriage to an artist.

Roy had conceived his plan a couple of months ago. Then he'd bugged Jenice's phone and Michael's phone, and even planted a bug in her purse. He was able to learn all about their plans to find the sunken gold, even down to the actual day they planned on looking for it. It seemed to fit the bill perfectly for his plan.

Roy was acquainted with the dealings of Stuart Fox from some of his crime reporter friends. He figured it would be a simple matter to lure Fox into a "hunt-for-gold" scheme. He'd simply use Fox to get Jenice away from Michael and to set up the adventure he needed. It was a wild idea and one Roy would never have considered if he had seen any other way of breaking her and Michael up. But—he could think of no other way.

From the beginning, the plan was to entice Stuart into bringing Jenice and him here to this island. Roy knew he could engineer an escape from the yacht, especially since he had it figured to win Stuart's confidence well in advance. Roy was good at that sort of thing, and he knew he could catch Stuart unaware. Once he and Jenice were alone on the island, he could make his play.

Roy had every angle figured, including their eventual escape from this island. He'd even had a boat hidden on the island for that purpose. The boat was in place now, all gassed up and ready to go. There it would stay, safely tucked away while he worked things out with Jenice. Then, once he had things under control, he'd simply make a lucky discovery by happening onto the boat. No doubt about it, he had covered all the necessary ground. Nothing could go wrong. Nothing at all.

Roy looked over at Jenice. "Tell me something," he said, his voice soft and appealing. "What did you see in this Michael fellow that you didn't see in me?"

Jenice flushed and instantly her eyes glistened. "That isn't a fair thing to ask me right now, Roy. It's just not a good time."

"I, uh, didn't mean to be insensitive, Jenice. But I can't help wondering if you and your new friend might be less compatible than you think. Have you given it enough time? I mean, the man's an artist, for heaven's sake. You're an adventurous woman, Jenice. What sort of adventure could you ever expect from living with an artist? You could help him select a frame maybe or clean his brushes once a week."

"Roy, please!" Jenice pleaded. "I know you think you're looking out for my best interest, but this really isn't the time."

"When is the time, Jenice? If I didn't say something, and you ended up throwing your life away on this man, I'd never forgive myself. You know yourself how many times you've vowed never to give up your life of adventure just for the sake of marriage. Michael is the wrong man for you, Jenice. I think if you'll honestly consider all the possibilities, you'll see that I'm right."

Jenice brushed away a tear and stared at Roy. "Are you telling me you're the right man for me, Roy? Is that where this conversation is leading?"

Roy stood, walked to Jenice, and took hold of both of her hands. "You know I'm crazy about you, Jenice. And you know that you and I are just alike. Admit it, if it weren't for worrying about Michael, you'd be flying at the edge of the clouds being in the middle of this kidnapping thing."

Jenice's eyes lowered. "Maybe and maybe not, Roy. But I am worried about Michael, so it's a moot point anyway." She drew a quick breath, stood, and looked Roy directly in the eye. "We'd better move a little deeper into the island. Those guys will be looking for us any time now. We might as well make ourselves as hard to find as possible."

"Yeah," Roy said with a faint grin. He helped her up, and the two of them went on the move again.

They had traveled only a short distance when they broke through into a large clearing. Jenice couldn't believe what she saw. "Would you look at that?" she exclaimed. "It's the old house. The one Brad Douglas built while he was living here on the island."

"Hey, you're right. It is Brad's old house. Check it out, Jenice. It withstood that monstrous storm a lot better than I figured it could. For the most part, the place is still standing."

Jenice sighed. "Too bad we still don't have his generator in working condition. If we had electricity, we might get his old radio working. That way we could get some help."

A nervous surge crossed Roy's mind. Was there a chance that Brad's old radio might somehow be made to work? That would ruin everything.

"There is no electricity, Jenice," he quickly pointed out. "Why even speculate about such things?"

"What's with you, Roy? You sound like you're worried we might find a way to make the radio work. It's not like you to give up without a struggle. Come on, let's go inside and look at the radio. Who knows what we might come up with? We might even find a way to get it working, who knows?"

When Roy hesitated, Jenice decided to set out on her own. She took one step toward the house and suddenly froze in her tracks. It took only a second for Roy to realize her reason. A man was walking toward them. He had evidently come from the old house and was headed right in their direction.

Roy's heart jumped to his throat. "What is this?" he asked in total dismay. "There's not supposed to be anyone on this island."

* * *

Jenice stared at this man who had unexpectedly appeared out of the house. A chill shot through her as she realized he could be from the yacht. But—that made no sense at all. She had gotten a close look at all those men, and this wasn't one of them. This man stood a good six feet tall, had dark wavy hair, and a square-cut jaw that gave him a rugged handsomeness she might expect in a movie star. He walked with an air of dignity and radiated confidence. Everything about him indicated he was a man of wealth and position. "Hello, there," he called from only a few steps away.

Somehow this man seemed vaguely familiar, but she couldn't put her finger on why. It wasn't as if she knew him personally; it was more as if she had seen him in a magazine or maybe on television. She glanced over at Roy, who stood expressionless, just staring at the approaching man.

"I hope you'll excuse me for staring," the man continued. "I don't get many visitors on my island."

"Your island?" Roy gasped.

"I suppose it's not really my island, but since I'm the only one living here at the moment, it's only natural that I think of it as mine. And when I say I don't get many visitors, I'm not stretching things one bit. With the exception of a certain salty old sea captain, the faces have been quite scarce around here since I took up residence."

Salty old sea captain? Had Jenice heard right? Could it be that the famed ghost of Captain Horatio Symington Blake was still haunting this island, and that this newcomer—whoever he was—had encountered the ghost? The same ghost that she herself had encountered the day she was here on this island with Michael? Her reporter's instincts tempted her to pursue the matter further, but considering the other, more pressing matters confronting her, she let it go.

The man extended his hand to her. "May I ask your name?"

Jenice set aside thoughts of Captain Blake and accepted his hand. "Jenice Anderson," she responded, "and this is Roy Jenkins." After another moment studying the man's face, she remarked, "Excuse me for saying this, but you look very familiar. Is there a chance we've met?"

With a slight smile, the man shook his head. "No, I don't believe we've met," he responded. "You may have heard of me, however. My name is Howard Placard. I'm . . ." He paused, then corrected himself. "That is to say, I *was* a major motion picture producer. That is . . . before certain things happened to change everything."

Jenice blinked in surprise. "Howard Placard?" she repeated, amazed to learn that this man was the well-known tycoon motion picture producer. "Yes, I have heard of you, Mr. Placard. I've even been a guest on your private beach a couple of times."

Howard gave a hollow laugh. "I'm afraid I don't own the beach any more. I don't own much of anything, other than what you can find on this island." His eyes held a faraway look. "Or should I call it a prison? That's more what it is for me, I'm afraid. A prison without walls."

"What a strange thing to say about this lovely island," Jenice remarked. "Why would you refer to it as a prison?"

Howard drew a quick breath and expelled it loudly. "I'm afraid it's a very long story. In a nutshell, I was accused of some illegal dealings with the IRS. Actually, I was framed, but I was under the gun, nevertheless." He sighed. "To put it bluntly, I faced a prison term. I was offered a deal. If I agreed to spend five years on this island as my punishment, I'd be spared a possible ten-year term in a federal prison. So you see, this island is my prison. Sorry to say I hate everything about it, but I'm stuck here." He paused a moment. "Now, may I ask what brings you to this island?"

"Hmmm . . . , you have an interesting story, Mr. Placard," Jenice commented. "I've never heard of anyone being sentenced to a prison term on an island before. It sounds to me like you managed the better of the two evils, if a federal prison was the only other choice."

"Yes, much as I hate to admit it, I do agree. This is better than prison."

"You ask what brings us here." She laughed. "We have a bit of a strange story, too. Are you sure you want to hear it?"

"Please, I'd really like to hear. You have to understand, my daily routine is not all that jam-packed with excitement these days. Having visitors on my island is a remarkable treat. I'd love to know what brings you here."

"All right," Jenice agreed. "You gave us your story in a nutshell; here's ours. Roy and I were abducted by a bunch of hoodlums who held us prisoner aboard their yacht. We managed to escape when they anchored just off the north shore. But they will be coming ashore looking for us once they realize we're gone. Which brings up a question. Do you possibly have access to a phone, or a two-way radio, or any means of communication with the outside world?"

Howard's expression turned to one of interest and concern. "I noticed a yacht anchored off the north end of the island earlier this morning."

"That's the one," Jenice said quickly.

"Hmmm. Drug runners, I'd guess."

"We think so, but we're not positive. One way or another, they are bad guys of the worst sort. How about that phone? Do you have one, Mr. Placard?"

"I'm sorry, Miss Anderson. I wish I could help, but I have no means of communication with the outside world at all. How did you happen to get mixed up with this bunch, if I might ask?"

Roy spoke up for the first time. "Jenice and I are reporters, and these guys figured we were onto them. I'm hoping we can hide out on this island long enough for them to give up finding us."

"That may not be necessary, Mr. Jenkins. I have no means of communication with the outside world, but I do happen to have access to a boat."

"You own a boat?" Jenice asked, her voice filled with anticipation.

"No, I don't actually own a boat," Howard corrected "What I said was, I have access to a boat."

A horrified look crossed Roy's face. "What do you mean, you have access to a boat?"

"Actually it's a bit of a mystery even to me. About a week ago some people arrived in two boats. They left one tied up on the south end of the island. Then they just took off. I have no explanation at all for this. But it's true, the boat is there."

* * *

Roy's eyes widened and great beads of perspiration formed on his brow as he nervously shifted his weight from one leg to the other. What sort of rotten luck had brought this man to this island at this particular time? And what sort of rotten luck allowed him to spot the boat that Roy had paid to have hidden on the island? It wasn't fair. Roy had gone over every detail of his plan. But how could he have possibly foreseen this development? Since Jenice knew about the boat, she would naturally want to jump in it and head for the mainland as soon as possible. That would completely foil his plans of having time to persuade her over to his way of thinking.

Roy felt the front pocket of his trousers. A slight smile crossed his lips as he assured himself the keys were there. Howard Placard might know where the boat lay hidden, but without the keys the boat would be useless. Roy was no dummy. He had left strict instructions that no keys be left with the boat. This part of his plan was still workable. The boat would be useless until Roy determined it was time to make it usable. When the time came, he could miraculously find the keys. It would be easy to convince Jenice someone had dropped them near the boat.

Howard Placard was another matter altogether. Running into the man was definitely a setback. Still, Roy prided himself on being one to make the most of any situation. Okay, so he had a couple of obstacles in his way. No big deal. He'd have Jenice talked out of her wedding plans right on schedule. Then the way would be open for him to get her into a white dress just for him. After all, the two of them were meant for each other. Anyone with half an eye could see that.

* * *

"How big is the boat?" Jenice asked. "Big enough to get us to the mainland?"

"Yes, I'd say so," Howard responded. "As long as the weather holds out. And right now there appears to be no sign of bad weather approaching."

"You know, Mr. Placard," Roy thoughtfully said. "There's something that bothers me. You think of yourself as a prisoner on this island. If, in fact, you do have a boat at your disposal, why not use it yourself to make your own escape?"

"That's a very good question, Mr. Jenkins. And the answer is simple. If I should try to escape this island, the . . . uh . . . person who banished me here would be on my back like a tiger on its prey. I'd have a new address in a heartbeat. And I'd have a new view, looking out a postage-stamp-sized window with iron bars on it. No, Mr. Jenkins, I won't be needing the boat to make my escape. It's all yours. Now, would you like me to take you to it?"

CHAPTER 14

Darwell didn't know what had hit him. One second everything was normal, and the next—everything went berserk. The blades on the chopper froze in place, the people inside became like Egyptian mummies, and all the sounds that had been pounding in his ears went silent. Dead silent. This was eerie. More eerie than anything Darwell had ever experienced. He glanced back at the patrol. Everything in that direction was frozen in place as well. It was almost like looking at a Norman Rockwell painting instead of real life.

"What in the blue thunder is going on here?" he growled. "Somebody's playing games, and I don't like games. Heads are going to roll when I find out what this is all about."

Darwell's next big surprise came in the form of a female voice. "Don't get yourself all excited, Detective. It's only me. I have time on hold at the moment."

He spun to see her standing no more than three feet away. Instinctively, he raised his gun. "Whoa there, lady. How'd you sneak up on me like that? Bad mistake. It could get you shot."

"I don't think so," Samantha smiled. "Not unless your finger has a bullet in it."

"WHAT?!" Darwell cried, looking at his empty hand where the borrowed revolver should have been. "Twice in one day? What is going on here?"

"Don't worry about it, Detective. You won't be needing the gun, so I simply returned it to the officer you borrowed it from."

Darwell glared at his empty hand and then at this strange woman who stood grinning at him. "Who are you?!" he demanded. "And what's your game?!"

"My name's Sam. And I'm here to pick a bone with you, Darwell. Michael happens to be my brother, and I'm not happy with the way you've been hounding him."

"You're this guy's sister?" Darwell snapped. "I wouldn't be too proud of that right about now if I were you, lady. This guy is treading deep water. And while we're at it, how is it you know my name?"

Samantha chuckled. "I know a lot more about you than just your name, Darwell. And take my word for it, it's not my brother who's treading water. It's you, slick."

Darwell's eyebrows furrowed. He took another look around at the motionless scene surrounding him. "Let me ask you a question," he said finally. "Are you by chance in cahoots with a truck driver who goes by the name of Gus?"

"I know who you mean," Samantha laughed. "Gus and I go way back. Not to say I don't get a little aggravated with the guy now and then. But—I always get over it."

"I thought so. This Gus pulled a strange trick on me earlier this afternoon. Swapped out my gun for a kid's plastic pistol. I still can't figure how he did it. Can't put a finger on how you're managing this little show of your own either. You have to understand, sister, I'm from Miami. It takes a lot to rattle my cage. And don't think you're out the door scot-free. I plan to see to it that you pay the piper for whatever you're up to with this little dog and pony show."

Samantha laughed. "If I were you, Darwell, I'd stick to playing Dick Tracy and leave the stand-up comic routines to guys like Jay Leno. Now, I suggest you get a good hold on your badge, Detective. We're going on a little journey."

Darwell's eyes narrowed. "A journey, you say? The only journey we'll be taking is a trip downtown in my squad car." Darwell removed the handcuffs from his belt and took a step toward Samantha. "You have the right to remain silent. Anything you say can, and will, be used against you."

That's as far as Darwell got. It all happened so fast, he didn't know what hit him. Over the years, he had been on a lot of roller coasters, but never one quite like the invisible roller coaster he found himself on now. He was swished up, down, around, and through twisting turns, hills, and spiraling loops that defied all description.

When all movement stopped, he found himself suspended in midair overlooking an ocean that stretched to the horizon in every direction. The woman was right beside him. He glanced at her, he glanced at the cuffs still in his hand, and he glanced again at the precarious situation he found himself in.

"You've slipped me some drugs," he accused her. "I don't know how you did it, but you've given me drugs."

"No drugs, Darwell," Samantha assured him. "There are thousands of ways to move into a holographical playback, but in your case I wanted to add a little extra fun to the game. So I included a few dramatics. I figured it was only fitting since you obviously have a flare for the dramatic. What else could you call the idea of trying to put a Special Conditions Coordinator in handcuffs?"

"Special Conditions Coordinator? There's that term again. That's what your cohort Gus called himself. What? Are the two of you members of the same street gang?"

"Back off, Darwell. You're pushing me, and I get agitated when I'm pushed. Take my word for it, you won't like me when I'm agitated. Now do me a favor. Take a look at that boat down there, right below where you're hanging."

Darwell gathered his wits and glanced straight down. She was right about the boat being there, but the boat was the least of his concerns at the moment. He was thinking too clearly to be high on any drug she may have slipped him. So there had to be another explanation for all this. But what?

"If I'm not on drugs," he pressed, "how are you holding us up here like a couple of box kites? You're a crafty one, lady. I know this is an illusion, but you've got my mind spinning trying to decipher it."

"Strike two, Darwell. You're not on drugs and this is no illusion. It's what we Special Conditions Coordinators refer to as an enhanced holographical replay. What you're about to see actually took place yesterday. But—you'll get to see it exactly as it happened. You should count yourself lucky; not many on your side of the line ever get to experience one of these. Come on, I'll take you in a little closer to the scene so you can have a better view."

Darwell held his breath as he and Samantha slowly descended toward the boat. It was sort of like being in a glass-enclosed elevator on the side of a towering building. Darwell had encountered every conceivable kind of bad guy over his years on the force, or so he had thought before this caper. If anything ever could bring thoughts of early retirement, he was experiencing it now. As they came within only a few feet of the boat, their descent ceased and they again hovered inexplicably. It was then that Darwell caught sight of the two people on the boat, a man and a woman. It was the man who demanded his attention.

"It's him!" Darwell shouted. "The guy that's been eluding me!" Darwell glanced back at Samantha. "Your brother!"

"My, aren't we the observant one?" Samantha granted with a hint of sarcasm. "Why do you think I'm treating you to this replay? I want you to see for yourself how those drugs got on my brother's person. Hopefully, seeing the truth will penetrate that thick skull of yours enough to unlock your stubborn mind-set." Samantha pointed to the north. "You see that small spot on the horizon over there?" she asked.

Darwell shoved the handcuffs in his pocket and shielded his eyes with his hand to look. "I see it. So what?"

"Just keep watching. You're about to get a close look at the faces of the real culprits you should be chasing, instead of wasting your time harassing my brother."

By this time, Darwell realized the spot Samantha had pointed out was in reality an approaching boat. He found himself overcome with another strange phenomenon, perhaps the strangest yet. He realized that he was feeling the fear and apprehension being emitted from the two people on the boat just below him.

"What is this?" he asked. "How can I know what those people are feeling? There ain't no way."

"Oh, did I forget to mention this part of the holographic replay? It is a little mind-boggling, isn't it, Detective? In this sort of replay, you get to feel what the people involved were actually feeling when the event took place. It's a whole lot better than just trying to pick some face out of a lineup, eh, slick?"

Darwell glared at Samantha. Never in his life had he been in a position of such helplessness. He was one who delighted in taking charge of any situation. Grave resentment boiled within him toward this woman who held him literally captive to her will. This was humiliation to the core of the word's meaning. His jaw tightened as he continued watching the impending scene unfold.

"Who do you think they are, Michael?" the woman on the boat asked nervously.

"I'm not sure, but from their looks I'd say they're up to no good."

The woman spoke again. *"What do you think? Should we make a run for it?"*

"Not in this boat. Those guys could run circles around us. I hear tell these waters are notorious for drug runners, but I can't imagine what they might want with us."

The seriousness of what he was seeing penetrated Darwell with unbelievable force. Try as he would, there was no shaking off the effect it was having on him. He swallowed his pride and looked again at the woman who held him captive in her web of inconceivable magic. "This is all real, isn't it?" he made himself ask.

Samantha smiled warmly, and her whole countenance softened. "Yes, Detective Darwell, it is real. You're looking at the scene that put Michael in the hospital. Just keep watching. I told you he was innocent; now you can see for yourself."

Darwell looked again at the approaching boat. If what he was seeing was real, he could only guess this boat was manned by the true culprits in this case.

"You there!" one of the men on the approaching craft yelled. *"Pull up. We wanna talk."*

Darwell observed two men on the forward deck of the intruding craft. One was armed with a short-barreled shotgun and the other a pistol. "I know those guys," Darwell grunted. "I've seen their mug shots. The one with the shotgun is Max Yorty. The other is Lefty Nelson. These cockroaches are into drugs so deep they're lower than a gopher in my Aunt Hilda's cabbage patch."

"You got 'em pegged," Samantha affirmed.

Darwell strained to see more of what was happening on the boats. By this time Michael had brought his craft to a stop, and Max and Lefty had stepped aboard.

"What do you want from us?" Michael asked, staring down the barrel of the shotgun.

"Did you hear that, Lefty? He's asking what it is we want. Why do

you suppose he would do that?"

"Don't rightly know, Max. Could have something to with the way you're tickling his tonsils with the barrel of that shotgun."

Both men let out a burst of crude laughter. Then Max said, *"Rumor has it the two of you are in a possession of a certain map. I want that map and how I get it makes little difference to me. We can do this the easy way, or we can do it the hard way. If we do it the easy way, the two of you can be about your business. On the other hand, if you choose the hard way you might find yourselves facing a few problems I'm sure you'd rather not face. Either way I get the map. So what'll it be. The easy way, or . . . ?"*

"What's going on here?' Darwell asked. "It would appear your brother and this lady have a map showing the location of something valuable."

"Yes," Samantha said. "There is a map. And it does show the location of a rare and valuable treasure. A treasure that rightfully belongs to Michael."

"And these men want to steal the map?"

"Right on, Detective. I'll move the replay forward a few minutes to spare you all the unnecessary details."

Darwell heard a shot. He looked quickly to see it had been fired by a third man who remained on the intruder's boat. "That's Stuart Fox!" Darwell cried out, seeing the man who had fired the shot. "The guy's a con man to the core. He's invented more stings than a river has ripples. I want this slug bad. Trouble is, I catch him and some high-powered lawyer puts him back on the street." Darwell slammed a closed fist into his other hand. "There's nothing I have less use for than a scheming lawyer who keeps bad guys on the streets."

Darwell turned his attention back to the replay as he watched Jenice rush to where Michael had fallen. *"MICHAEL!"* she screamed, cradling his head in her arms. *"WHAT HAVE YOU DONE? YOU'VE KILLED HIM!"*

"Bring the lady," Stuart Fox instructed calmly. *"We'll plant some stuff on the body and leave him in the boat. That way when they find him they'll figure he was taken out in drug deal gone bad."*

"That's how it happened?" Darwell mused aloud. "That's how our boy got shot?" He looked at Samantha. "I've misjudged your brother," he admitted. "I'd have bet Daddy's old red underwear your Michael was a drug runner."

"I'm glad to see you're man enough to admit your mistake," Samantha grinned.

"No!" Jenice cried. *"You can't just leave him here like this! He needs help!"*

Max took hold of Jenice's arm and pulled her up. *"Forget him, lady. He's beyond help now. And that's what's going to happen to you, too, if you don't produce the map we're looking for."*

Struggling was of little use as Lefty joined Max in manhandling Jenice away from Michael and onto their waiting boat. There her hands were pulled behind her and handcuffs applied.

"Now why'd you guys have to go and do that?" Darwell asked, while exhaling a long sigh. "I hate it when I see a woman mistreated. That won't go good when we come face to face, believe it, slugs." His eyes remained glued to the scene as Max returned to Michael's boat. There he went over everything on Michael's person as well as the boat in general. Michael's wallet was taken, and a package was placed in his right hand. Darwell recognized it as the package of crack he had labeled as evidence.

"I don't know how you're pulling this off, Sam," Darwell said, admitting she had a name for the first time. "But however it's done, this is the greatest tool for the justice system I've ever laid eyes on. I don't suppose you could help me out with a few more of my cases, could you? Maybe even drag a judge or two along for the ride?"

"Sorry, Detective," Samantha responded. "Michael and Jenice are not only family, their names also appear in my office files. It's my responsibility to insure a certain contract between the two of them is honored. That's why I've been given the approval to work with you on this case. I wish I could help with some of your others, but . . ."

Darwell took courage. "Look, uh, Sam. I'd have to be blind not to see you're no ordinary woman. I don't know what term best describes you, but you're anything but ordinary."

"Try calling me an angel," she smiled. "That'll do nicely."

"An angel?" Darwell's mouth dropped open and he covered his mouth with his hand, then blew out a loud breath. "This isn't easy for a man of my position, but angel it is if that's what you tell me. Let's, uh, see if we can cut some sort of deal here, Angel Sam. What do you say?"

"You want to cut a deal with me?" Samantha asked, shocked at his audacity. "You do realize I'm the one in the driver's seat here, don't you?"

"You have the upper hand at the moment, I'll give you that. But what's the hurt in turning what's happening here into something that will benefit the both of us?"

Samantha raised an eyebrow. "Your point is?"

"My point is, you want your brother's name cleared. I want the gang of drug runners that's been eluding me for months. And I want Stuart Fox off the streets for good. I can clear your brother's name with one phone call, which I'll gladly make if you'll help me. You're a powerful woman, Angel Sam, hands down. If Curtis Darwell can be shoved in a corner with no more effort than you put out, what sweet-talking lawyer would ever stand the chance of a rabbit in an eagle's claw against you? That's my point. You scratch my back, and you know the rest."

Samantha broke out laughing. "You are one gutsy guy," she said. "I'd say Miami's bad guys would do wise to cut you a wide path."

Darwell eyed her for a long moment. He pressed his luck. "One more little thing, Angel Sam," he ventured. "My gun, the one your friend Gus relieved me of. May I have it back? I like that gun."

Samantha laughed so hard it brought tears. "You know who you remind me of?" she asked. "No, of course you don't. You couldn't possibly know my uncle J.T MacGregor. But so help me, you're the first man I ever met with a gutsy stubborn streak to match his. Check your holster."

Darwell reached inside his jacket and checked. A smile crossed his lips. The gun was there. "Can I take it this means we have a deal, Angel Sam?"

Samantha nodded affirmatively. "Yes, Curtis Darwell, we do have a deal. I've got some cleaning up to do, and working with a man like you might just make my job a heck of a lot easier. We need to sit down and discuss our tactics. Which brings up a question, slick. Your office—or mine?"

CHAPTER 15

Jenice was astounded at how much easier walking through the rain forest was behind someone who knew the established trails. The growth was so thick in places, one could be only feet from the trail and never know it. With Howard leading them, the trip from Brad's old house to the south beach took less than a third the time it took Jenice and Roy to find the house coming from the north beach.

As they broke through the last of the underbrush onto the south beach, Howard spoke up. Jenice was a little shaken by his comment. "I couldn't help notice the engagement ring on your finger, Miss Anderson. May I take it that you and Roy here are more than just friends?"

Howard's words brought back thoughts of Michael. Pictures of his motionless body lying alone in the boat on the Atlantic haunted her thoughts with bitter intensity. But she refused to give up hope. Michael was alive. She just knew he was alive. The realization that Howard was leading them to a boat that could take her off this island to where she could learn for a surety of Michael's fate buoyed that hope.

"Ha!" She heard Roy laugh halfheartedly. "I wish. The lady here did wear my ring once upon a time, but the ring you see on her finger now isn't mine."

Jenice added, "Actually, Howard, I'm engaged to marry Michael Allen. Roy and I are the best of friends, and we've worked together for several years. But—"

Roy cut in. "That about sums it up," he said. "Except to say I'm still available should things not work out with Mr. Allen."

"Well," Howard responded, a sadness filling his eyes. "It's been my experience not to hang many hopes on waiting for a lady to ask another man to hit the road. I've had a little experience at that game myself." He exhaled loudly. "I apologize for putting my nose where it didn't belong. It was thoughtless of me."

"Not at all," Jenice corrected him. "You had no way of knowing."

"Up the beach, around the bend ahead, there's a cove." Howard pointed to his left. "That's where the boat is."

"What are we waiting for?" Jenice asked, moving out briskly in the direction Howard had indicated.

Roy hung behind as the other two scurried away. He kicked angrily at the sand and mumbled something inaudible under his breath. At last he followed behind them.

* * *

"Boss!" Max yelled. "Take a look at this! I found 'em. It's that Jenkins fellow and the broad. And get this, there's another guy with 'em."

Stuart had been searching the island in a different direction through his own binoculars. When Max cried out, he instantly spun around to see where Max was pointing. "Down there, on that stretch of beach to the south," Max elaborated. "And it looks like they're in a hurry to get someplace."

Stuart raised his binoculars to look for himself. "Bingo, Max!" he shouted. "We got 'em! I knew this lookout point would be our best bet." Stuart zoomed in on Howard. "We got bigger problems than I thought, Max. It would seem Jenkins isn't alone in his double cross. He's brought in help. I don't like the looks of this, not one bit."

"Let's get back to the boat, boss. We can nab 'em before they know we're on to them."

"No, you fool! By the time we got back to the boat and to the south beach, they could be anywhere on this island. Let's stay right here and watch for the time being. They're up to something, Max. And unless I miss my guess, what they're up to is retrieving a hidden map."

"The map? Yeah, boss, that's right. They're after the map."

"And once we know where the map is . . ."

"We're gonna be rich," Max sneered.

Stuart panned the area ahead of the three. He could see they were headed for a part of the beach that was just out of sight from the vantage point where he and Max were now. "Keep an eye on them, Max," he said. "I'm going to move to the other side of this lava rock so I can get a better view of the area where they're headed to. Whatever we do, we can't afford to lose sight of them."

Suddenly, they heard a noise in the distance to the north. "What's that?" Max gasped.

"It's a helicopter," Stuart came back. "There, see. Just over the treetops."

"Yeah," Max agreed. "Is it the cops?"

"No, it's military. Nothing to worry about. Just some flyboys out on maneuvers."

As the two men watched, the helicopter made a turn toward the west. Max looked worried. "They're headed right to where our boat's docked, boss. What if they see it?"

"So what if they do see it, Max? They're just a bunch of flyboys getting their hours in. They couldn't care less about a boat anchored on this island. Now keep an eye on our friends down there. I'll move a few yards farther inland so I can have a good view of where they're headed."

* * *

Howard had no problem leading Roy and Jenice to the boat. Once there, he removed the rigging holding the canvas cover in place. With Roy's help, they had the canvas removed in no time at all.

"All right!" Jenice cried exuberantly. The boat was a little smaller than the one she and Michael had made the dive from, but it was definitely large enough for her purpose. "We can easily make Miami in this boat," she observed.

"Miami?" Howard quizzed. "Wouldn't it be better to go to Saint Thomas Island? It's much closer than the mainland."

"No!" Jenice countered without the slightest hesitation. "If Michael's alive, he'll be in Miami. I just know it. Miami is our target."

Howard continued his argument. "You could catch a plane from Saint Thomas, Miss Anderson. That would put you in Miami faster than using this boat."

"You're forgetting one thing, Mr. Placard. Roy and I are both victims of a kidnapping. There's bound to be an alert out for Roy, possibly for me, too. The minute we hit Saint Thomas, we take the chance of ending up in a web of government red tape. No telling how long we might be delayed. I'm not chancing it; we head straight for Miami."

"I see," Howard conceded with a nod. "You do have a point at that. Well, this boat has everything you need to get you to the mainland. Water, dry rations, plenty of fuel, everything. Whoever brought the boat here left it readied for a quick trip somewhere. Again, I suspect we're dealing with drug people. I don't know who else would leave a boat here like this."

Roy stepped up to the boat and gave the inside a once over. "I, uh, hate to bring this up," he said, doing his best to sound sincere. "But there are no keys in the ignition. We can't get very far without the keys, can we?" He quickly covered his mouth to hide the smile he was unable to prevent.

"No keys?" Jenice responded, glancing at the empty ignition switch. "I don't believe this. There must be keys here someplace. Maybe they're hidden somewhere in the boat." Quickly, she climbed inside where she began a thorough search of every nook and cranny in the boat.

* * *

Max was just catching up to Stuart where Stuart had settled in at his new vantage point. "I lost 'em back there, boss. Ya got 'em from here?"

"I see them all right, Max," Stuart explained worriedly. "But I don't like what I see. I don't like it one bit. They have a boat. They're fixing to make a run for it, Max."

"A boat?!" Max gasped, quickly raising his own binoculars. "We got to stop 'em, boss. If they get away, we'll lose a fortune."

"They're not going to get away, Max. Get on the radio and call Lefty. Tell him what's going on here. Have him bring the yacht around to a point where he can keep an eye on these guys until we can get back to our boat. We'll have no trouble overtaking that little rig, just so long as we know where they are."

Max broke out the radio and called Lefty. He quickly brought him up to speed on what was going on with Roy, Jenice, and this third man who had shown up out of nowhere. He ended the transmission by passing on Stuart's order for Lefty to bring the yacht into surveillance position.

"All right, Max," Stuart said, once the radio transmission was done. "It's time we get back to the boat. We're about to pay a surprise visit to a couple of unsuspecting schemers."

* * *

"I'm sorry, Jenice," Roy said when she failed to find the missing keys. "It's no use. We can't get very far in this boat when we have no way to start the engine."

"No!" she shouted back. "There has to be a way. This boat is my only hope for getting to Michael. Help me look, Roy. Those keys have to be here someplace."

The concern in Roy's eyes was real. Whatever he was, he wasn't a cold-hearted monster. His heart ached seeing Jenice like this, but he was sure that what she felt for this Michael fellow was only infatuation. If he could only stall her long enough to work a little of his own magic, he was sure he could win her love again. After all, she had changed her mind about marrying someone else a couple of times before. If Roy could just keep Jenice here a little longer on this romantic island and if he could only get Mr. Placard out of the picture, he was sure he would win back her heart.

"Jenice," he said, hoping to calm her without giving up on his lie. "No one would leave a boat unattended with the keys in it. It's no use, the boat will do us no good."

Jenice was crying now. Roy loved her so much he hated seeing her cry. It angered him all the more that Stuart Fox had been so callous as to shoot Michael down in cold blood. Convincing Jenice she really wasn't in love with Michael would have been much easier if she didn't think he was lying wounded in some hospital.

"This isn't like you, Roy," Jenice lambasted him. "Get in here and help me look for those keys. They have to be hidden here someplace, I just know it."

Roy sighed. "Tell her, will you, Mr. Placard? The keys aren't going to be here. Whoever left this boat here certainly didn't intend to make it easy for someone to steal the thing."

Howard turned to look at Roy. Roy felt the weight of suspicion in the big man's eyes. Even though Roy hadn't mentioned it, he knew more about Howard Placard than he had let on. Roy was a reporter, and a good reporter knows about celebrities such as Howard Placard. Roy knew of Howard's infatuation with Lori Douglas, the wife of one of his movie directors. It was common knowledge how Howard had made a fool of himself trying to steal Lori away from Brad Douglas, Lori's husband. What Roy was doing, right now, wasn't all that different from what Howard had done, and he was almost certain Howard knew. True, Jenice wasn't married to Michael yet, but their wedding date was set.

Roy tried to get a grip on himself. This was all foolishness. Howard couldn't possibly know these things. It was Roy's guilt making him feel this way. In spite of everything, his guilt refused to soften. Still, he wouldn't give up on his purpose. Not with Jenice at stake, he wouldn't.

"No, I'm sure there won't be any keys," Howard said, agreeing with Roy's observation. This brought a brief smile to Roy's lips. But the smile quickly faded as he watched Howard join Jenice in the boat. Once there, he moved quickly to the driver's seat and proceeded to work the throttle back and forth a few times. Roy couldn't believe it when Howard reached under the dash and flipped one of two switches mounted there. Howard depressed the second switch which brought the sound of a grinding starter. Seconds later the engine caught hold and roared to life.

Roy's mouth fell open. Howard Placard had obviously checked the boat out ahead of time and had somehow figured a way of wiring around the ignition switch. It wasn't fair! It just wasn't fair!

"All right!" Jenice cried out at hearing the engine start. "Miami, here we come!"

"How did you do that?" Roy asked meekly, his shaking voice pitched an octave higher than usual.

Howard laughed. "I only said I wouldn't use this boat to escape the island, I never said I wouldn't take it for a joy ride or two. You see, Roy, there's a side to Howard Placard most people don't know about. I haven't always been a movie producer. I was raised on my father's ranch in Arizona. When I was around fifteen, Dad had an old tractor he was about to haul to the dump. I begged him to give it to me. He told me I could have it if I kept it up, so it didn't become an eyesore around the place."

Howard paused, letting the memory focus in his mind before going on. "I painted that old relic with five coats of red lacquer and polished it once a month every month. I rebuilt the engine from the ground up and kept it in top running condition." Howard grinned. "As for the keys? They were lost long before I got possession of the thing. I just wired a couple of switches around the ignition. One to turn the thing on and off, the other to engage the starter. Changing the wiring on this boat was a snap. I had all the tools and parts I needed, thanks to Brad Douglas. Brad left stuff on this island you wouldn't believe."

Roy only shook his head. Howard Placard of all people? Who would have believed him capable of hot-wiring a boat?

Howard continued his story. "Living on this island can be pretty darn boring, as you can well imagine. As I explained earlier, I have no plans to escape from this island, but taking this boat out for a couple of joy rides is the most fun I've had since being banned here. Oh, and if you're worried about the gas I used, I refilled the tank from the supply of gas Brad left on the island. He used it to run his generator."

Roy needed a new plan, and he needed one quick. There was no way of keeping Jenice here on the island now, not with a workable boat at her disposal. But that didn't have to be the total setback it seemed on the surface. If Roy could keep Jenice distracted enough that she didn't notice which way he was navigating, he might just manage an unscheduled detour in his trek back to the mainland. There were any number of islands between here and Miami he could set ashore on. And with a little bit of luck, he might even figure a way to fake engine problems with the boat. It just might work. It had to work; it was his only hope. He took a few quick breaths to calm his nerves.

"All right," he said. "We'll put to sea and hope we slip unnoticed past the guys on the yacht. We can head west a few miles before turning north. That should keep us out of their sight long enough for us to make our escape."

* * *

Lefty Nelson grinned as he replaced the microphone to the hook on the shortwave radio. "So, our Mr. Roy Jenkins was more than just a guest on our yacht," he muttered to himself, contemplating what Max Yorty had just told him. "And now he's thinking he can pull a fast one. Too bad Max gets first shot at him. Nothing makes me sleep better at night than carving up some turkey like Jenkins."

Lefty walked to the control cab where one of the men was standing at the wheel. He was the one they called Slippery Jake. "Time to pull up anchor, Jake," Lefty told him. "We've got orders to swing around to the west side of the island. Looks like we may have a couple weasels in the hole, and the boss wants us to keep a short leash on them."

Jake eyed Lefty. "How about the map?" he quizzed. "Does Max have his hands on it, yet?"

"Max didn't mention the map, Jake. But I got a hunch it will be in our hands before the sun goes down tonight. I'm sure Stuart Fox thinks he's the one who has things under control, but so long as me and you boys are around, Max is holding all the aces. We're going to be rich men, my friend. And Stuart is going to be fish food."

"Yeah?" Jake grinned. "I figured you and Max had something cooked up. I was right, huh?"

"Me and Max are inseparable, Jake, you know that. We had this thing figured from the start. And you know whatever me and Max have, we share with you boys."

"Yeah," Jake grinned. "Just like always. That's why me and the boys take such good care of you and Max. Always have, always will."

Lefty grinned to himself. As long as he could keep these bilge rats satisfied with cheap talk, why not? "That's what teamwork is all about, Jake," he added. "Now get this yacht under way. We got a job to do."

* * *

Roy lifted the anchor, then moved to the driver's seat. He put the boat in gear in preparation for pulling it out of the backwaters. Jenice glanced over at Howard. "How can we ever repay your kindness, Mr. Placard?" she asked.

Howard smiled. "I'll tell you how," he said without the slightest hesitation. "When this is over, you can send me a care package. I haven't had a good meal in so long I've forgotten what it's like. Make it a Porterhouse, or a New York cut. A big one. A baked potato, lots of butter and sour cream—throw in the makings for a fresh garden salad—and a coconut cream pie." Howard closed his eyes and pictured the meal in his mind. After a moment, he opened his eyes and looked back at Jenice. "That's the way you can repay me," he said. "Right about now I'd give everything I own in this world for a meal like that."

"I'll go you one better, Mr. Placard," Jenice responded, smiling. "When this is all over, I'll personally hunt out the best chef in these parts and send him here to fix the meal for you."

"I'll be looking forward to it, Miss Anderson," Howard responded. "Godspeed to you both, and may you find your Michael alive and well."

Roy eased the throttle forward. The stern lowered into the water as the propeller caught hold. Slowly, the boat inched forward toward the open sea.

"Good-bye!" Howard called again, with a one-handed wave. "Good luck!"

"Good-bye, Mr. Placard," Jenice called back over the noise of the engine as Roy pushed the throttle ahead another notch. "And thank you so very much."

Once the small craft reached the open water, Roy jammed it into high speed. Jenice looked back at Howard, never taking her eyes off him as long as his lonely silhouette could still be seen against the background of the tiny island.

* * *

By the time Stuart and Max reached their boat, and headed it out to the open sea, Jenice and Roy had a healthy head start. They had not slipped away unnoticed as they had hoped to do, however. Lefty and his gang had them under surveillance from the time they pulled out of the island's cove.

"Ya want I should intercept 'em?" Lefty radioed to ask Stuart.

"No," Stuart instructed him. "Just hang back far enough so they don't notice you, and keep them in sight. Max and I will overtake them in this boat."

Though Stuart didn't give Lefty his specific reasons for wanting to intercept Jenice and Roy himself, he did have his reasons. Stuart was certain Jenice knew the whereabouts of the map even if she didn't have it in her possession And he had a plan for extracting the information out of her. A foolproof plan, the way he saw it. Jenice Anderson was a strong woman, he couldn't deny that. But she wasn't a murderer. And that little fact was Stuart's ace in the hole. Rather than allow Roy to die a slow painful death, she'd tell Stuart where to find the map. Then, once she revealed the location of the map, she would become expendable—just like Roy. Stuart didn't believe in leaving witnesses.

His plan didn't end there either. With these two out of the way, the only one knowing he had the location of the sunken treasure would be Max. Poor Max. Eradicating him was almost a shame. But, with Stuart, business was business. As soon as Max became a liability, he would have to be dealt with like any other liability.

* * *

For the first half hour neither Jenice nor Roy spoke. Roy was busy navigating the boat, and Jenice was swallowed up in her own thoughts about Michael. It was Roy who finally broke the silence. "I know you're worried about Michael," he said. "I can't blame you for that. But I think you should face some facts about your relationship with him. You can't afford to allow one fun-filled adventure to cloud your mind to what life would be like with Michael once that adventure is over."

Jenice stared at Roy. "What are you getting at?" she asked.

"I think you know what I'm getting at, Jenice. Michael's buried treasure. Yeah, I admit, that does offer up an adventure. One whale of an adventure. A sunken treasure from a three-hundred-year-old ship-wreck. A mysterious map leading to the location of the treasure. The thrill of discovery, and later on retrieval of the gold. It's all there, I can't begin to deny that. But what happens when the adventure is over? You can't kid me, Jenice. You're not interested in the money the gold will bring. Once that gold is in a safe somewhere, it won't mean any more to you than a pile of desert rocks would. And with that adventure gone, you're going to be stuck with an artist for a husband."

Jenice closed her eyes tightly and clenched both fists. "Stop it, Roy!" she said tensely. "You don't know what you're saying. Michael loves an adventure just as well as I do. And even if he didn't, I'd still love him. Why can't you see that?"

Roy shook his head. "Jenice, Jenice. How many times have we had this same conversation? You thought you were in love with Bruce Vincent, too. You came to your senses about him, just as you came to your senses about Michael once before. Wake up, lady. I'm the one who can make you happy. We're just alike, me and you. We would make a great man-and-wife news team."

"Roy, please!" Jenice begged.

But Roy kept at it. "You and Michael are misfits, Jenice. You wouldn't stay married to him a year. The first time you got an itch to do an article in the jungles of Africa and you had to stay home to watch him paint a fruit salad—that would end it. Admit it, Jenice. You're not in love with Michael. You're only infatuated with him because he has a map to the sunken treasure. I know you're worried about him now, and that's the way it should be. But you're not in love with him. Not now, not ever. When will you get that through your head?"

Roy's words hit Jenice with a searing force like nothing he had ever said to her before. It happened so fast, she didn't even have time to consider her own action. In one bound she was standing next to his seat. Her hand flew out, striking his face with a stinging slap that left his skin bright red. A look of astounding shock appeared in Roy's eyes as his hand moved up to touch his reddened face. In all their years working together, never had Jenice done such a thing. For a very long time he just stood there looking at her.

Jenice made no apology for what she had done, but she couldn't look Roy in the face any longer. She turned her back on him and lowered her eyes. All the tension of the last two days rose to the boiling point. Tears she could no longer hold in flooded to her eyes, and she wept bitterly.

* * *

It was at that instant when Roy knew. It was over for him. Jenice really was in love with Michael Allen, there was nothing he could do about it. It felt as if the scaffolding had been kicked out from under Roy's world, and it had come crashing down in a heap of rubble. Roy felt suddenly sick. His whole reason for living had forsaken him. His mind whirled in stunned confusion. What had he done wrong? How had he failed? How could he possibly go on living, knowing that Jenice belonged to another?

He reached out to touch her, but she pulled away. Then a strange thing happened. Roy forgot his own pain. His heart cried out for Jenice, and the hurt that was bringing these tears, a hurt he gradually realized was there because of him. What had he done? He had put her life in danger. He had been the one responsible for Michael being hurt—or possibly even killed. For the first time, the magnitude of what he had done became clear in his mind.

What was he to do? Could he keep the truth hidden from Jenice? No, that wasn't Roy's way. Keeping her in the dark for now was one thing. But even if his plan had worked, he would have told her the truth eventually.

Another thought struck him now. Not only did this mark the end of any hope for marrying Jenice, it also marked the end of a great friendship between them. Once Jenice knew, she could never forgive him. And even worse, he could never forgive himself.

The stinging on his face was nothing compared to the stinging in his heart. But now, for the first time, he knew what had to be done. He had to get this boat to the mainland the fastest way possible, and he had to help Jenice find Michael. Oh how he prayed that Michael would be alive.

Seeing that the boat was doing fine at the moment, he left it on its own and moved next to Jenice. "I—I'm sorry," he said, reaching for her shoulder but not quite touching it. "I was wrong, wasn't I? You are in love with him."

She lifted her head, but she didn't turn to face him. "Yes," she said coldly. "I am in love with him, Roy. What you said to me was cruel and something I never would have expected from you."

"Yes, it was cruel," he admitted. "And I am sorry. I'll get you to him, Jenice. I give you my word. I'll get you to him. And more than this, I'll dance at your wedding." He paused for several seconds, and then added, "If you'll still have me at your wedding, that is."

CHAPTER 16

Jenice turned and threw her arms around Roy. "Of course you're invited to my wedding," she sobbed. "There will always be a special bond between you and me, Roy, you know that. We have a friendship that goes far beyond our working relationship. We just don't have the chemistry between us for a marriage." Jenice backed away and looked at Roy through reddened eyes. "The chemistry that *is* there between Michael and me."

Roy smiled. It was a bit forced, but he smiled all the same. "Yeah," he said. "And I give you my promise never to make the mistake of not believing you again."

Suddenly, something caught Jenice's eye. It was a boat. One on a course to intercept their boat. "No!" she gasped. "It's them, Roy! The ones from the yacht. I recognize that boat. It's the one I was abducted in."

Roy turned to see for himself. "Of all the cursed luck!" he yelled. "It is them." He moved back to the driver's seat and shoved the throttle all the way open. "There's no way we can outrun them," he admitted. "But I might as well make it as hard as I can for them."

Reaching into his back pocket, he removed the pistol he had taken from Stuart when he and Jenice had escaped from the yacht. "Here," he said handing it to Jenice. "Hold onto this, just in case."

Jenice took the pistol from him. "Just in case?" she asked. "You think this little gun will stop them?"

"Probably not," Roy admitted. "But hold onto it anyway. You never know what might come up."

Jenice shoved the pistol in the back pocket of her jeans.

"Maybe we'll get lucky," Roy remarked. "Maybe a coast guard boat will come by to save us."

* * *

"Those fools have seen us," Stuart laughed. "They can't think their boat will stay ahead of us, Max. They're grasping for straws."

Max checked his shotgun to be sure both barrels were loaded. "Pull alongside, boss," he said. "I'll put a couple of shots across the bow. That should bring them to a halt."

Stuart narrowed his eyes. "I can make out two of them, Max. They must have left the other man on the island. No matter, it's the woman we want. She's the one who knows where the map is tucked away."

"How do you figure on making her talk?" Max quizzed. "She's a tough one, boss."

Stuart grinned. "Open the map box over there on your side, Max. In it you'll find a little plastic case."

Max opened the box and removed the case Stuart had described. "You mean this, boss?"

"That's it, Max. That just happens to be the lever we need to pry the information out of the lady. Stick it in your pocket, Max. We'll be needing it a little later on."

Max shrugged and shoved the case in his pocket. "Is that shotgun of yours loaded?" Stuart asked.

Max nodded. "Both barrels, boss."

"Good, keep it handy. I like your idea of firing across their bow. I'll be alongside them in less than two minutes at the rate we're going."

* * *

"Talk about déjà vu," Jenice said, as she watched the fast-approaching boat. "Didn't this just happen to me yesterday?"

"Not funny," Roy responded. "We've been in some scrapes together, lady, but I think this one tops the rest. The way I see it, we're in big trouble."

"You'll get no argument out of me on that one, Roy," Jenice agreed with a sigh. "But we'll find a way. We always find a way. And on the bright side, these are the guys who shot Michael. I was hoping to come face to face with them again. Of course, I was hoping to do it under a little less lopsided conditions."

The sound of Max's two shotgun blasts were not only deafening, they were also convincing enough for Roy to cut the throttle. Jenice watched as Max reloaded his gun and Stuart brought the larger boat to a stop next to the boat she and Roy were in. These were the only two men in sight on the boat, but she couldn't help remembering the last time when Stuart suddenly appeared from below deck. She vowed to keep her guard up a little better this time around.

"Well now," Stuart said, once the boats were secured together. "Decided to go for a boat ride, did we?"

Roy took the initiative. "Yeah, we did, Fox. It just seemed like the perfect day for it."

"Too bad you never know what might come along and spoil a perfect day like that, eh, Jenkins?"

"Yeah, too bad."

"Nice set of shiners you have there, Max," Jenice chided. "What did you do, run into a door?"

"Shut up, broad!" Max spit back. "You're gonna pay for these shiners, you can bet on it!"

Stuart waved Max off. "I'd like to offer the two of you an invitation to my boat," he said. "It's very comfortable, and I have a feeling it will be afloat a little longer than yours. Show them what I mean, will you, Max," Stuart said pointing at the bottom section on the smaller boat.

"Be glad to, boss," Max said, taking aim with his shotgun. Again the air was split with the sounds of two blasts, this time leaving two gaping holes in the bottom of the smaller boat. When water instantly began rushing in through the holes, Jenice and Roy wasted no time moving to the larger boat. It took less than three minutes for the damaged boat to slip below the surface of the water on the final leg of its final journey.

"Ah, that's a shame," Stuart snickered. "Don't build those little boats like they used to, I guess. One little bullet hole, and the darn things sink. Oh well, we won't be needing that boat any longer, anyway. This one is big enough for all of us."

"Keep these two covered, Max," Stuart said, holstering his gun and removing a leather pouch from his inside jacket pocket.

Max had reloaded again, so he pointed the shotgun in the general direction of Roy and Jenice. "Recognize this leather pouch, Miss Anderson?" Stuart said, dangling the pouch from its tie-string.

"I recognize it," she spit out. "Those are the gold coins you stole from me earlier."

"That's not nice, Miss Anderson. And let's don't say I stole them from you. Let's just say I got them from you in a business deal. What do you say?"

"In your dreams, dirtbag."

"Hmmm. Spunky as ever, I see. You know, Miss Anderson, these are some very rare coins. Not only are they rare, they're also proof positive that more just like them are lying on the floor of the Atlantic right now. I want the ones still on the floor of the Atlantic, Miss Anderson. And you know what, you have a map showing exactly where I can find them. Is my point coming through loud and clear?"

"Do me a favor, Fox," Jenice said coldly. "Drop dead."

Stuart paid no heed to her sarcasm. He merely went on with what he was saying. "I understand you and Roy were once engaged. How touching. I'm sure he still has feelings for you. The question is, do you still have feelings for him? Shall we find out?"

Jenice's action came so fast, Stuart had no chance to defend against it. With lightning speed she whirled into a spinning dropkick that landed squarely on Stuart's jaw. Next came an elbow to his midsection, which doubled him over in excruciating pain. Before he could recover, she yanked the leather pouch containing the twelve gold coins from his hand and held them only inches from his face.

"You shot the only man I ever loved!" she shouted. "And you expect me to reward you with a fortune in gold? Not hardly, Mr. Fox. You'll get no gold. Not even these coins you stole from me the last time we met."

"NOOOOOO!" Stuart screamed frantically as he watched her turn and throw the pouch into the dark Caribbean waters. Max lunged forward in an unsuccessful attempt to catch the pouch before it cleared the boat, but he was barely able to maintain enough balance to keep from falling overboard.

"You little witch!" Stuart growled, wiping the blood from his swollen lip. "Those coins were worth a small fortune. I ought to throw you in after them." Quickly evaluating his chances of overpowering this woman, obviously skilled in martial arts, Stuart revised his course of action. "Your shotgun, Max. Keep it trained on this crazy woman. If she so much as blinks, let her have it."

Max raised the gun. "Don't think I won't use this, lady," he grinned. "Not that I'm ready to kill you just yet. But it would be a shame to mess up either one of those lovely legs of yours, now wouldn't it?"

Stuart sucked in a long breath and pulled himself together. "So we lost a few coins," he grimaced. "There's plenty more where they came from. Hand me that little plastic case lying on the control panel, will you, Max?"

"You mean this, Fox?" Max asked, picking up a case.

"That's the one. Let me have it." Max handed him the case. Stuart made a point of opening it in such a way that both Jenice and Roy could see the contents clearly. The case contained a hypodermic needle and two vials of clear liquid. One of the vials was marked with a strip of red tape, the other was marked with green. "Do either of you have any idea what this is?" he asked menacingly.

Neither Jenice nor Roy answered.

"No?" Stuart mocked. "Well, let me enlighten you. This is a little experimental serum I happened to come across in some of my dealings recently." He removed the vial with the red marking. Jenice watched with guarded interest as he shoved the needle into the vial and filled it by drawing back slowly on the plunger. "One shot of this serum and the recipient has less than an hour to live." Stuart removed the second vial, the one marked green, and held it up for all to see. "Unless, that is, you receive the antidote that is in this little bottle." This second vial he slid into his shirt pocket. "Hold the shotgun steady, Max," he said, moving closer to Roy. "We wouldn't want anyone to play hero needlessly, now would we?"

Stuart stepped directly in front of Roy. "Roll up your sleeve!" he snapped. Roy didn't move. "Do it now, Jenkins, or I'll give Max the green light. Maybe a leg, maybe an arm. Either way you won't like it much. Now roll up that sleeve."

Roy looked first at Max's shotgun, then at the needle in Stuart's hand. "I have a bit of a problem here, Jenice," he said slowly, although there was very little fear showing in his voice. "I don't suppose you might consider telling them where the map is, by chance?"

Jenice threw her head back defiantly. "Why, so they could just kill us both on the spot? Forget it, Fox. Do what you will with either or both of us. You'll never see one ink spot off that map. If I go to my grave, the whereabouts of the gold goes with me."

"Yeah, that's what I thought you'd say," Roy responded. "I'd have been disappointed if you'd said anything else."

"Roll up your sleeve!" Stuart shouted through clenched teeth. "Let's get this party in swing."

Roy suddenly stood very erect and took on a new demeanor. Jenice couldn't help but notice. Now he seemed like the old Roy she had come to know so well over their years working together.

"Kill me if you will, Fox," Roy spit out. "It won't get you one thing from this lady. If you think I'm the one she cares about, you're dead wrong. I know that now. I should have known from the beginning."

Roy's chest rose and fell with each slow, deliberate breath, and he turned to face Jenice. "I'm sorry Jenice. It looks like I've made an unbelievable mess of things, thanks to my stupidity. I honestly believed I could win you back, and I certainly didn't intend for Michael to be hurt in the bargain."

Jenice felt a sudden throbbing in her head as the meaning of Roy's words began sinking in. "What are you saying, Roy?" she gasped.

"I'm saying I used this bunch of cutthroat thieves to set up your kidnapping, Jenice. I figured if the two of us had the chance to work together again, under the most dangerous of conditions, it just might wake you up to the fact that marrying Michael Allen was wrong for you. When I learned about you and Michael going after the gold, I concocted a plan. I wanted it to appear that these culprits had kidnapped us both in an effort to pry the location of the map out of you, but I knew you would never give in to their pressure. I had our escape planned from the beginning, and I honestly thought we could pull it off. I still think we could have if we hadn't run into Howard Placard. My idea was for us to hide out on the island long enough for these guys to let down their guard. The boat Howard led us to was mine. I had it stashed there for a getaway later on."

"You did all this trying to convince me not to marry Michael?" Jenice asked unbelievingly.

"Yes, Jenice. That was my intention."

"And the gold? You just naturally took for granted I'd share that with you, too, eh, Roy?"

"Believe me, I couldn't care less about the gold. That's why I made sure these apes didn't happen onto you while you were diving for the gold. I purposely planted a short-range tracking device on your boat for that very reason."

"You planted a tracking device on our boat?" Jenice asked. "That's how they found us?"

Roy hung his head. "I realize now it was a mistake. But I did make certain these men didn't learn where your treasure is hidden. What I wanted was the chance to win you back. I figured if that happened, the gold wouldn't matter all that much to you, either. Adventure is what we love, Jenice. Not a fortune in gold."

Jenice looked on in disbelief as Roy continued. "I had no idea these men were capable of murder. Maybe it was because I wanted you back so bad I closed my eyes to too many things. I'm sorry, Jenice. I know how empty this all must sound now, but I am truly sorry. I'd gladly give my own life if it would bring Michael back safely to you." He paused and sighed heavily. "I can't do that, but I can die to keep you alive. They won't kill you as long as you hold the secret to the whereabouts of the map. Make a deal with them, Jenice. Make sure you have your freedom before they get the map. It's your only chance. And you deserve to live."

Tears flooded Jenice's eyes. "How could you, Roy?" she gasped, sobbing softly. "How could you?"

Roy looked up; his eyes met Stuart's. In one deliberate motion, he rolled up his sleeve. "Go ahead, Fox. Get it over with."

Stuart laughed again. "You bore me with your theatrics, Jenkins. If you think it will save you, think again." Stuart jammed the needle hard into the flesh of Roy's upper arm. Once he had injected the liquid, he removed the needle and shifted his attention to Jenice. "You have ten minutes at most to save this man's life. The choice is yours."

Stuart returned the needle and red vial to the plastic case, which he tossed on top of a deck chair. He then removed the second vial from his pocket and rolled it tauntingly between his thumb and fingers. "This serum will counteract the poison, but it has to be injected within minutes. Tell me where the map is, and I'll let you both live. Keep silent, and Roy dies on the spot. You, on the other hand, Ms. Anderson, will live to make Max a little happier man. And Max does have a way of getting ugly while enjoying his work."

* * *

At first, Max thought it was his imagination, but by the third or fourth time he heard it, he wasn't so sure. Whatever it was, it was coming from down the stairwell that led to the bottom section of the boat. It sounded almost like a muffled whistle. He glanced down into the shadowy stairwell, straining to see anything out of the ordinary. There was nothing. The sound was real, he was sure of that. Could it be a mouse? Or perhaps a noisy bearing from one of the boat's mechanical parts? He glanced over at Stuart who had his back turned. Satisfying himself that Stuart had everything under control with these two, Max eased his way down the stairs keeping the shotgun pointed directly in front of him. Reaching the bottom of the stairs, he paused, letting his eyes become accustomed to the dimmer light.

Everything happened so quickly he was caught completely off guard. From out of nowhere a hand shot out grabbing the shotgun and ripping it from his grasp. The next thing he knew, he was hurled to the floor with a resounding thud. Before he could cry out, a large rag was shoved in his mouth. His hands were forced behind his back, and the sound of snapping handcuffs struck his ears with sickening force.

His mind whirled in confusion. Who had done this? Then it hit him. The guy who helped Roy and Jenice with the lifeboat—was it possible . . . ? Could the man have somehow managed to sneak onboard this boat? Max had to find a way to warn Stuart. But how? His feet were securely tied, his hands hobbled uselessly behind his back, and even his head was buried between a pair of pillows. He couldn't so much as tap a finger against the side of the boat to raise a warning. Whoever had done this had made certain of that.

* * *

Stuart rudely poked his finger into Roy's chest. "You're finished, Jenkins," he snarled. "And you know what? I'm going to savor every second watching you writhe in agony as your time winds down. You really thought you could play me for a sucker? Ha! You're a bigger fool than I had you pegged for."

Roy turned his head and looked away. "Why don't you shut up, Fox? Haven't you done enough without forcing me to listen to your senseless babbling?"

"No, Jenkins. It's not enough just to watch you die. I want to see you suffer first. I want you to picture in your mind what's going to happen to your girlfriend, here after you're gone. Believe me, Jenkins, it won't be pretty. And you're only kidding yourself if you think she won't tell us where the map is. She'll break her silence, all right. Max has his ways of loosening stubborn tongues."

Roy turned back to look at him, fire blazing in his eyes. His jaw tightened. "You're a loser, Fox," he spit out. "And you're going down. I only regret that I won't be there to see it."

"I'm going down?" Stuart scoffed. "In your dreams, pal. Don't forget, I was smart enough to catch you trying to run out on me. You can bet what little life you have left that I'm smart enough to cover my backside, Jenkins."

"Oh, you're going down, all right, Fox. I guarantee it. And when you do, just remember I predicted it. Let the sound of my final words ring out as your epitaph."

Stuart's lip curled into a bitter snarl. In a slow, deliberate move, he pulled the automatic pistol from his shoulder holster. Pressing the barrel hard against Roy's head, he cocked back the hammer with his thumb. "Maybe you'd like me to pull this trigger right now," he smirked. For several seconds he let the gun remain, then in one quick motion pulled it away and released the hammer. "No deal, pal. That would be too quick. You're going out slow and hard. And I'm going to enjoy every second of the show."

Though Jenice wasn't oblivious to what Stuart was saying, something else had caught her attention. Her eyes remained riveted to the open stairwell where she had watched Max disappear only seconds earlier. She, too, had heard the whistle-like sounds from below deck, which Roy and Stuart had apparently missed so intently were they speaking to each other. Jenice strained to hear anything further from the stairwell opening. There was a faint thumping, followed by some sounds that might indicate a struggle, then silence. She was certain something had taken place below the deck, but she had no way of knowing what.

As she stared into the shadows, a dark figure suddenly appeared. The light was too poor for her to make out his features, but it was definitely a man. It wasn't Max. This man was larger than Max, and whoever he was he must have noticed she had seen him. Very quietly, he raised a finger, which he pointed at Stuart. Then he gave a quick motion indicating he wanted her help in getting Stuart a little closer to the stairwell. Jenice hesitated only a moment. What did she have to lose?

"Let me ask you a question, Stuart," she said, staring him straight in the eye. "What are you going to do when I take that gun away from you and shove it down your throat?"

"Ha!" Stuart scoffed. "You won't try any of your Chuck Norris antics on me as long as Max has that shotgun aimed your way. You may be a fool, but you're not stupid."

"Oh? You think it's me who's the fool? Maybe you should take a glance backward and see just where Max does have that shotgun pointed. Or better yet, maybe you should just look to see if Max is still there at all. You might be in for a bit of a shock, Stuart."

"Please, Ms. Anderson. Don't even attempt something this trite. Give me credit for a little common sense."

Jenice smiled. "Max?" she called out. "If you're there, speak up."

The grin faded from Stuart's face when there was no answer from Max. "Max!" he called out, himself. "Where are you? Answer me, Max!"

Jenice posed her hands in a martial art's stance. "Care to look for yourself," she taunted. "Or do you dare?"

Beads of perspiration popped out on Stuart's forehead. Very carefully, he took three large and decisive steps backwards. This was precisely what she wanted him to do, since it put him in a position only a short distance from the figure in the stairwell.

Having distanced himself from Jenice, Stuart grabbed a quick look backwards. "Max!" he cried out again. "Where are you? This is no time for playing games! Get out here now! I need you, Max!"

Jenice took one step forward. Stuart spun pointing the pistol at her. "Hold it right there, Anderson!" he shouted. "I will kill you if I have to. Map or no map."

"I don't think so, slick," came a deep, gravelly voice from the stairwell. "I'm betting I could take the head off your shoulders without you ever getting off a shot."

Stuart spun to see who had spoken. As he looked on in complete shock, a large man in a tan overcoat stepped out of the shadows and into plain view. He was holding the biggest handgun Stuart had ever seen, and it was pointed right between Stuart's eyes.

"Let me introduce myself," the big man said. "Name's Darwell. Detective Curtis Darwell to you. And you know what, slick? The way I figure it, you got just about two seconds to lose the gun."

"Curtis Darwell?" Stuart smirked, moving his own gun around to point it at the detective. "I've heard about you, cop. They say you're good."

"I'm better than good, slick. I'm your worst nightmare."

"How'd you get in my boat without my knowing?"

"Doesn't matter how. It only matters that I'm here. Lose the gun, Fox. I'm growing tired of looking at you."

Stuart's hand shot to his shirt pocket, and he quickly retrieved the green-labeled vial. "Back off, Darwell," he said coldly, holding the vial up so it could be clearly seen. "If you were on the boat, then you obviously know this man will be dead in a matter of minutes without this antidote. You're the one who's going to lose the gun, pal. So help me, I have no problem smashing this vial. No problem at all."

No one was more surprised than Jenice at what happened next. Her ears rang as the sound of Darwell's discharging pistol reached

them. The vial in Stuart's hand exploded, showering the deck behind
him with shreds of splintered glass and spraying liquid. Stuart
screamed in agony as he pulled his bleeding hand close to his body so
he could examine it. The bullet had missed his hand, but the shat-
tered glass had done a number on him. "You're insane!" he shouted at
Darwell. "Do you know what you've done?"

"You picked the wrong guy to toss threats at, slick. I don't make
deals with bad guys."

Jenice couldn't believe any of this. "You do know what that vial
contained that you just destroyed, don't you, Detective?" she asked.

Darwell moved neither his eyes nor his gun, which were both
still focused on Stuart Fox. "I know exactly what was in the vial,
Miss Anderson," Darwell replied. "Fact is, *you* don't know what was
in it. Nor does our friend Stuart Fox here. You see, I just happened
to have some advance knowledge of the two vials Fox had in the
little plastic case. Not only that, I also had access to the vials while
Stuart was out traipsing around on the island spying on you folks.
That's when I switched the colored bands on the vials. You see, Fox,"
Darwell informed him, a slight smile crossing his lips. "The stuff you
injected in Jenkins was the antidote. He's not in trouble at all. But
looking at the blood on your fingers, I have to ask, did enough of the
real poison get in your bloodstream to cause your death? I'm betting
it did, slick."

Darwell reached over with his free hand and picked up the plastic
case containing the first vial and the hypodermic needle. "Now it's
you who needs a shot of the antidote within the next few minutes.
Care to argue further, or would you like to lose that gun now?"

A look of horror filled Stuart's eyes. He glanced again at his
bleeding hand, then at the plastic case Darwell was holding. He was
wise enough to know that enough of the poison must have entered
his bloodstream to put him in danger. He also knew there was still
enough antidote left in the unbroken vial to save him. In his stupor,
he looked first to Darwell, then to Jenice, and at last he let his eyes
shift to Jenkins.

Jenkins threw back his head and laughed. "You injected me with
the antidote? And you called me the fool? I think you should listen to
the detective, Fox. Lose the gun, and he might just let you live."

Stuart's shoulders sagged in recognition of his humiliating surrender. Releasing the gun, he let it drop to the floor at his feet. "Good move, slick," Darwell said, still holding his own gun steady. "Now kick it over here nice and easy."

Stuart placed a foot on the weapon and gave it a shove. Darwell closed the cover on the plastic case and tossed it to Stuart, who made a desperate effort to catch it. Darwell then leaned down and picked up Stuart's gun, which he slipped into his pocket.

It took Stuart only seconds to fill the needle and inject himself with the antidote. "Hope you don't mind sharing a needle with Jenkins, here," Darwell grinned. "But I suppose being sanitary is the least of your worries about now, eh, Fox?" Darwell stepped forward and shoved the gun right under Stuart's nose. "I guess you know what I want next, don't you, slick?"

Stuart returned the vial and needle to the case, which he closed and tossed aside. He didn't bother answering Darwell's question, instead he slowly turned his back on the man and put his hands behind him.

"Good," Darwell said. "We know the routine. It's always nice when the bad guys go down quietly. Saves me bullets, too. They make me buy my own when I'm forced to shoot some uncooperative schmuck. I hate it when that happens." Darwell shoved his gun in its holster, and snapped a set of cuffs on Stuart.

"I gotta know, Darwell," the dejected man said. "How'd you pull it off?"

Darwell laughed. "I got a silent partner, slick. Name's Sam. It seems Sam has been keeping an eye on you for some time now. Knows just about all there is to know about you. It seems that Sam and I came to an understanding. She took me to her office, and what an office it was. There we laid out the plans to bring you and your bunch of thugs down. It was a great plan, too. Remember the chopper fly-by, back on the island, when you and your crony, Max were standing on the lava rock? Sure you do, slick. Well, the chopper wasn't there by accident, friend. That chopper just happened to be my taxi. Let me off not ten feet from your boat."

"But? How did you know? How did this Sam that you mentioned know?"

Darwell laughed again. "How did we know? Now that's a pretty darn good question. Do you believe in angels, Fox? Because if you don't, you really ought to check into the subject a little deeper."

Stuart slowly turned so he was facing Darwell. "Give me a break here, will you. You got me hands down. Be straight with me, how did you know?"

"I told you, slick. It was an angel. A very lovely lady angel."

Stuart's face twisted into a look of fury. "Have your fun while you can, Darwell. You may have the cuffs on me now, but I'll be a free man with one phone call. I have lawyers in my pocket that will bury you so deep even the gophers won't be able to find you."

"Oh, I don't think so, slick. Ever hear of the TV program 'Smile—You're on Candid Camera'? Take a peek right over there, on the flagpole at the back of the boat. See anything unusual?"

Stuart wasn't the only one to look, Jenice's head jerked around instantly. She couldn't believe it. Right there on the flag pole, big as life, there was a video camera. Why hadn't she noticed before?

"What is this?!" Stuart demanded. "Who put that there?"

Darwell shrugged. "The lady angel put it there. You know, the same lady angel who put me onto you, slick. And you know what else? She's also furnished me with some other tapes. I have videos of you intercepting Miss Anderson and her friend's boat yesterday morning. I have an excellent view of you shooting Mr. Allen. Plus, I have tapes of your conversation with Miss Anderson on your yacht."

This brought something to mind for Jenice. She pulled the pistol from her back pocket and handed it to Detective Darwell. "Here," she said. "This is the gun that Stuart used to shoot Michael. You might like to add it to your list of evidence."

"You bet I would, Miss Anderson," Darwell said taking the gun from her. "I make it a habit never to turn down evidence."

Stuart glared at them. "You got nothing, Darwell!" he screamed. "You can't prove that gun is mine, and there were no cameras. You're lying through your teeth."

"No, I'm not lying. I have a hard time believing it myself, but it is a fact, Jack. The way the angel explained it, they have some pretty sophisticated cameras on her side of the line. Have them positioned almost everywhere it would seem. It was a simple matter for her to make copies for me. Not only that, she's even offered to be the prosecuting attorney in your case. Behind the scenes, of course. But let me assure you, slick, none of the lawyers you have in your pocket can compete with the agenda she has prepared. I like the way Roy here put it—you're going down, pal. You're going down hard. Oh, and by the way, Max and the other goons are going down with you." Darwell glanced at his watch. "As a matter of fact, they're going down just about now. That part of the plan is in the hands of a helicopter pilot and a couple of folks I just met."

CHAPTER 17

Seated in the helicopter, Shannon glanced at her watch. "It's three-fifteen, Tom," she said. "Time for our part of this little plan."

Tom nodded. "Yeah," he said. "But I have to admit, I feel a little strange playing the role of a police officer. I've flown missions in hot spots all over the world; I've come under enemy fire and I've returned the enemy's fire. But that was all strictly military. These guys we're after now are civilian drug runners, not enemy soldiers. It's just a little different, that's all."

"You have nothing to worry about Tom," Randall, the pilot, called back to Tom. "I contacted my colonel back at the base. He did some checking on this guy, Max Yorty, and his partner, Lefty Nelson. They both have records longer than a drill sergeant's duty list. Detective Curtis Darwell checks out, too. Bottom line, we've been given the green light to go after these guys. Just think of yourself as a rent-a-cop, Tom."

Tom drew a quick breath. "Anything to make the streets of Miami a little safer for our civilian population, eh, Randall?"

"Something like that, yeah."

"I hope things are going well on Darwell's end. We're at least in the safety of our helicopter; Darwell's down there right in the middle of things, playing foot soldier, you might say."

Shannon laughed. "I wouldn't worry about Curtis Darwell," she observed. "I'd worry more about any bad guy unlucky enough to come up against him."

Tom rubbed his chin. "Speaking of that cop, I never saw anyone do more of an about-face than him. One second he's out to nab

Michael Allen, the next second he's Michael Allen's strongest ally. Do you really believe him when he said he talked with an angel?"

"I do, Tom," Shannon confidently answered. "I happen to know this particular angel is real. She's the same one who helped out my brother, Brad."

Tom reached over and patted Shannon's hand. "If you believe in the angel Sam, that's good enough for me. Make sure you're strapped in tight. I gotta go up front with Randall now." Picking up the bullhorn Darwell had left in the chopper, Tom moved to the front seat next to the pilot. "How do you feel about angels, Randall?" he asked.

Randall glanced over at Tom. "Never seen one, exactly," he explained. "But I can vouch to having a few in the seat next to me without fear or shame. And believe me, they've always been welcome passengers." Randall was silent a moment, then added, "My dad was helicopter pilot in Vietnam. He tells of a time when he had the help of an angel in saving the life of a downed pilot. So you'll get no argument out of me about an angel bringing on Darwell's change of heart."

"Okay, Randall," Tom grinned. "Let's get on with it, what do you say?"

Randall signaled a thumbs-up, then swung the chopper around on a course heading straight for the yacht. Tom stared at the bullhorn in his lap and drew in a deep breath. No doubt about it, for him at least, dealing with angels was a new experience.

* * *

Jake was still at the wheel of the yacht with Lefty at his side when something caught his eye. "Hey," he said pointing toward the sky. "Look here. I think we got company. There's a chopper heading straight for us, boss. Up there, see it?"

Lefty shielded his eyes with a hand. "Yeah, I think you're right, Jake. He is headed our way. No need for worry this time around, though," he laughed. "For once in our lives, we're clean."

Jake stroked his beard nervously. "We're not quite clean, boss," he confessed uneasily. "Some of the guys weren't too happy with the idea of putting all our apples in one cart."

Lefty eyed him suspiciously. "What are you trying to say, Jake?"

"I'm saying there's a stash on board. Hidden away in one of the lifeboats. We just sort of figured—you know . . ." Jake shifted his weight from one leg to the other.

"You figured what Max and me didn't know wouldn't get you hurt, is that it, Jake?"

"Yeah, sorta."

Lefty yanked off his ball cap and slapped Jake hard across the face with the back of it. "You idiot! How much stuff is there?"

Jake's Adam's apple bobbed up and down as he swallowed three or four times. "Enough to bring a hundred G's on the street," he allowed.

"Idiot! Idiot! Idiot!" Lefty shouted striking Jake with the cap again. "You know the word was we stay clean for this operation! I ought to throw you overboard along with the rest of your brain-dead cohorts. Which brings up the question. How many of the others are in on this little game of yours?"

"All five of 'em, boss. Like I said, we just didn't put much stock in this sunken treasure thing, and we didn't want to make no wasted trip."

Lefty glanced again at the approaching chopper. By now, he could see that it was a military and not a police craft. "You better hope those guys are just out for a joyride," he snapped bitterly. "Getting rid of a lifeboat full of crack in broad daylight won't be easy."

As the sound of the chopper grew louder, the five remaining men came one by one to the front of the yacht to join Lefty and Jake. The looks on their faces left no doubt as to what was going on in each of their minds.

Seconds later, the chopper was hovering directly overhead. A man leaned out holding a bullhorn. "HOLD IT RIGHT THERE, GENTLEMEN!" he ordered. "THERE'S A POLICE BOAT HEADING YOUR WAY AT THIS VERY MOMENT. THEY'RE UNDER THE COMMAND OF A DETECTIVE CURTIS DARWELL." There was a short pause, and then came, "MAYBE YOU'VE HEARD OF HIM, EH?!"

"What do we do, boss?" Jake quizzed tensely, never taking his eyes off the chopper.

"What do we do?" Lefty shouted back. "What do you think we do? We make a run for it! Our only hope is to stay ahead of these guys long enough to dump the stuff over the side without it being seen."

A look of apprehension crossed Jake's face. "How we gonna do that?" he asked.

"I don't know how we're going to do that, but we're darn sure not surrendering to Curtis Darwell's boys. I know that man's reputation. We make a run for it and do our best to dump the stuff."

Lefty shoved the throttle full open and cranked the wheel, bringing the yacht to an easterly heading. This put the yacht on a course bound for the open Atlantic.

* * *

Randall laughed. "Looks like our boys are a little hard of hearing down there. What do you think, Tom?"

"Maybe we should speak a little louder, Randall. You suppose that might help?"

"What the heck, we can try."

Randall brought the chopper into position and fired off a burst of machine gun fire directly in front of the yacht. Tom pointed the bull-horn back at them and yelled, "OTHER WAY, GUYS. WHAT DO YOU SAY?"

Randall maneuvered to a position where the chopper was directly facing the yacht. They were so close they could see the frightened expression on the culprits' faces as they all stared right into the barrel of the chopper's machine guns. The yacht slowed, and after a moment, turned, taking up a direction that put them dead on course toward the police boats just now coming into sight.

* * *

"Cut me some slack, Lefty," Jake pleaded. "The boys and me had no idea we was gonna run up against the U.S. Air Force."

"Shut up!" Lefty snapped. "And don't think you're going to get a Christmas card from me this year, because you ain't!"

* * *

Stuart turned ash-gray as Darwell shoved him down on the bench at the edge of the boat. He stared, unbelievingly, up at the camera on the flag pole.

Jenice's mind was racing. What Darwell had said opened up a huge question. "Let me ask you, Detective," she boldly ventured. "This lady angel you mentioned? Did she by chance claim to have a brother named Michael?"

"You nailed it, lady," Darwell smiled. "And unless I miss my guess you've got a few other things figured out right about now."

"He's alive," she gasped. "Michael's alive, isn't he? If Sam's on the job, I refuse to believe anything else." Her eyes aglow with excitement, she grabbed the lapels of Darwell's coat. "He is alive, and you know where he is, don't you?"

Darwell shot a thumb toward the stairwell, but didn't say a word.

Jenice shifted her eyes to the stairwell. Her hand flew to her mouth as she gasped in surprise. "Michael? Is it really you?"

Michael stepped out of the stairwell and walked straight to Jenice. Cupping her face in his hands, he said softly, "It's me, baby. I'm very much alive. And thanks to Sam and the good detective here, you're safe now, too."

Jenice reached out and removed the Dallas Cowboy cap from Michael's head, revealing his bandage. Very gently she touched it, then lowered her hand to caress his face. For several seconds, she let her fingers run over the contours of his face. "It's true—you are alive."

"I'm alive," he grinned, "but take it easy on the head, okay. Thanks to that jerk over there, I've still got one massive headache."

She stepped back and examined him from head to toe. "What are you doing in those clothes?" she asked. "And those boots? Have you turned cowboy on me in the time we've been apart?"

Michael laughed. "You can't believe what I've been through since we've been apart. The boots are the very least of my story."

Slowly, Jenice's arms encircled his neck. "We can get to your story later," she told him. Then, pulling him to her, she kissed his lips ever so softly. "How did you manage to find me?" she whispered. "It was Sam's doing, wasn't it?"

"Oh yes," he assured her. "Detective Darwell here was on me like a bloodhound until she showed up. Sam convinced him of the error of his ways, then the two of them got together and devised a plan. Sam put the detective in a helicopter with me where he explained the plan to me and to a couple of others who were along for the ride. You remember Shannon Douglas, don't you?"

"Sure, I remember Shannon," Jenice responded. "Was she in on the plan, too?"

"She was, along with her friend Tom Reddings. They were both a big help."

Jenice brushed away a tear and kissed him again. "Remind me to thank them next time I see them," she said, her voice cracking with emotion. She buried her face deep in his chest. "I guess you know I thought you were dead, don't you?"

"Yeah, I figured you did. But as you can see, I'm still alive and kicking. Cowboy boots and all."

This struck her funny, and she laughed. As she did, she noticed Darwell just preparing to snap the cuffs on Roy. "Wait, Detective," she said giving Michael's hand a squeeze and then stepping over to the other two men. It was a toss-up who had the greater look of surprise—Darwell or Jenkins. Darwell's eyes narrowed as he stared at her. "I gotta cuff him, ma'am. I heard his confession the same as you," he said gruffly.

"Please, Detective, just let me speak with him first."

Darwell shrugged and took a step backward. Roy swallowed hard and just looked at Jenice.

"Tell me the truth, Roy," Jenice began. "Your confession was a lie concocted to protect me, wasn't it? The truth is, you've been working undercover trying to put these guys away, isn't it?"

Roy ran a hand through his hair and shook his head. "Jenice, I—"

"Roy!" she cut him off. "You and I have had some great adventures together. We've always come out on top in the end. Just like now. Look around you. Stuart and his gang are going away where they won't bother the honest people of society ever again. And Michael is okay. Thanks to his sister. Let me make myself clear. This little adventure will be the last you and I ever share. Would you want me to go through my life thinking badly about you for not coming clean and telling your part in this thing just the way it happened? Or would you rather I have fond memories of our last adventure?" Placing her hand on his shoulder, she repeated, "You've been working undercover with this gang, and you lied trying to protect me. That's how it happened, isn't it, Roy?"

For a long time, he said nothing. He just returned her look, eyes filled with a combination of shame and gratitude. His chest heaved with a deep breath. "Yes, that's how it was. I was working undercover. I lied about my part in the plan, trying to protect you, Jenice."

She smiled, then leaned in and placed a light kiss on his cheek. "That's what I thought, Roy. I'm going to miss working with you, but you have to understand, I have a new partner now."

"I know," he whispered. "Michael is a lucky man. Thank you, Jenice. For everything."

For a moment longer she stood smiling at him. Then she walked back to Michael and put her arm through his. "No need for the cuffs, Detective," she said. "Roy's on the same side you are."

"You're sure about this?" Darwell questioned one final time.

"You heard him, Detective. He's a journalist—like me—and he was working undercover on this case. You can't very well arrest him for helping to catch this gang of thugs, can you?"

Darwell put the cuffs away. "You got a point there, lady. Even if I did run this guy in, he'd end up with a suspended sentence, facing a month of community service. What the heck, slick. Get out of my sight."

CHAPTER 18

Michael pulled Jenice around to face him. "I have a proposal for you, lady," he said. "What do you say we catch the first plane back home and get on with our wedding plans?"

Jenice placed her finger to Michael's lips and softly traced their outline. "Best idea I've heard since I decided to marry you in the first place, Michael Allen. Let's do it."

"I guess my idea of hunting the gold before we were married didn't turn out very well, did it?"

"Did too," she teased. "How much more adventure could either of us have hoped for? This is something we can tell the grandkids about."

"What a wonderful bedtime story," Michael chuckled. "Grandma was kidnapped, Grandad was shot in the head . . ."

"And they all lived happily ever after," Jenice cut in with a pinch to his cheek.

Something caught Jenice's eye. "Well, I'll be," she said in surprise. "Captain Horatio Symington Blake? Is it really you?" The captain was standing just behind Michael, who turned to see him also.

"Aye, lassie, it be me."

"Don't tell me you've been instrumental in watching out for Michael through his ordeal?"

"Aye, that I have."

"Well thank you, Captain Blake. Had I known he was in your capable hands, I never would have been worried."

"I gotta admit," Michael said. "The captain did look after me pretty close. I'd have been in a pickle without him."

"It's been me pleasure, matey," Blake smiled. "But I'll be biddin' ye farewell now. Ye be in good hands, says I. Godspeed to ye, me good friend. And may the tides be with ye."

A lump formed in Michael's throat as he waved good-bye to this good friend. A friend who had helped him through one of the biggest challenges of his life. "Good-bye old friend," he said.

"And good luck to you," Jenice added.

The captain offered a brisk salute and a very wide smile, and then—just like that—he was gone.

Jenice looked around to see Darwell, Roy, and Stuart looking at her with varying degrees of questioning expressions on their faces. She ignored them and lay her head on Michael's shoulder. "I lost my memory, you know," he whispered in her ear.

Her head jerked up in surprise. "You what?" she asked.

"I lost my memory," he repeated. "And you know what finally brought it all back to me?" She shook her head and he smiled. "Hearing your name," he said softly.

She lay her head against his shoulder once again and snuggled in closer to him. "I love you, Michael Allen," she said without the slightest hint of reservation. "I thought I'd lost you, and now that I have you back, I'll never stop saying I love you again."

"And I love you, too, Jenice Anderson. I do now and I always will." He kissed her cheek. "And don't think I don't know how difficult it is for you to say you love me. But that's okay. It makes it all the better when you do."

Roy spoke up. "I'm going to miss working with you, Jenice," he said. "But I know now you're where you belong."

"Yes I am, Roy," she responded. "I'm exactly where I belong."

Roy swallowed away the lump in his throat. "If it's not too much bother, could I ask just one favor? Would you think of me once in a while?"

She smiled at him. "You know I will, Roy."

Roy turned to Michael. "You're a lucky man, Michael," he said. "You have no idea what I'd give to be in your shoes. You take care of this lady, you hear me?"

"You don't need to worry about that, Roy," Michael answered. "I will."

Jenice turned Michael's face back toward her and kissed him. "Thank you, Michael," she said. "Thank you for understanding me and for not dying on me. Thank you for coming to my rescue and for being a man who loves adventure. And most of all, thank you for loving me."

"You're welcome," Michael said. And he returned her kiss.

* * *

Tom Reddings shut off his cell phone and smiled. "Looks like everything is secured," he said. "The police have the men from the yacht in custody, and Darwell tells me he has the others in hand. Take us home, Randall."

The pilot acknowledged his words with a wave and turned the chopper back toward Miami. Tom had left his seat in the front of the chopper and moved back to sit next to Shannon. He reached out and took her hand. "What do you think?" he asked. "Did you get some good material for your next novel?"

"Yes, Mr. Tom Reddings, I did," she answered. "And I'm glad everything turned out well for Michael and Jenice. They're good people."

"Tell me," Tom teased, "are you going to include the part about the angels in your next story?"

Shannon laughed. "I believe in angels, Tom, but I don't write about them. Mystery novels are my thing. Why don't we leave the subject of angel novels to certain other authors, okay?"

"Okay with me, my dear Miss Shannon. But do you suppose one of those certain other authors might come up with a story about us some time? Maybe we could have an angel or two help us work out a future together?"

Shannon leaned over and kissed Tom. "Wouldn't surprise me a bit, my handsome pilot." she said. "Not one bit."

* * *

Unknown to any in the chopper, two more passengers were seated in the back seat; they simply chose not to make themselves visible at the moment. Jason laughed. "From the look on your face I'd say Shannon's prediction might not be too far from your mind, Sam. Am I right?"

"I haven't actually looked far enough ahead into our future files to know for sure, but like she said—it wouldn't surprise me."

"I have to admit, Sam. You did a good job cleaning this one up. Michael and Jenice are making all their final plans for the big moment, Captain Blake is back on the island babysitting Howard, and Darwell is wearing a smile that an industrial-size eraser couldn't wipe off."

"Ha!" Samantha laughed. "Darwell ought to be smiling after all the evidence I put in his hands. By the time Stuart and his gang get back on the streets of society, they'll be too old to deal in any drugs stronger than Geritol. Darwell kept his part of the bargain, too," she grinned. "Michael's name is whiter than Frosty the Snowman on Christmas Eve. Yes, I'd say this case is pretty much history. All that's left is for me to go shopping for a new dress to wear to Michael's wedding and reception."

Jason's brow furrowed. "Sam. You're not thinking of showing ourselves at the wedding? The higher authorities aren't going to approve that."

"We don't have to show ourselves, Jason, I know that's against the rules. But we are going to be there. He is my brother, you know."

Jason shrugged. "I agree we should be there. But why a new dress if no one will see us?"

Samantha stared at her husband, as if unable to comprehend how he could even ask such a question. "How could you think I'd go to my brother's wedding and reception in an old dress? You're wearing a tux, too. So don't even think about arguing with me."

Jason shrugged. "Right you are, Sam. A new dress for you and a tux for me."

"I swear, Jason Hackett. Sometimes you can be so insensitive. I don't know what I'm going to do with you."

"Insensitive am I?" Jason responded, his face suddenly lit up with a boyish grin. "I'll bet Howard Placard would argue that point with you right about now."

"Howard Placard?" Samantha asked. "What do you mean, Jason? You've lost me."

"You're the one who told me about Howard's request for a special dinner, remember?"

"Oh yeah," Samantha laughed. "You're referring to his asking Jenice to send him a care package, I'm guessing. I wonder what Jenice is planning to arrange for him."

Jason's eyes twinkled. "Jenice promised to send Howard the best chef she could find, didn't she? Need I say more?"

"Well I'll be darned, Mr. Hackett," Samantha conceded, reading his meaning loud and clear. "Maybe I was wrong about your being insensitive after all, my crazy little ghost."

* * *

Howard Placard stood looking in disbelief at the table prepared before him. He had never seen such a feast. It smelled heavenly. He looked back to Captain Blake and asked again, "Jason Hackett did this just for me?"

"Aye, matey, that he did. He heard yer request for a decent meal, says I, and he was glad to oblige. Take me word for it, laddie, ye'll never be tastin' vittles like these again. Not for a long season, says I."

Blake was right. It was a meal like none Howard had tasted before, even with the power of yesterday's wealth to buy the best chefs in any land. He breathed deeply and glanced across the moonlit beach as a white-capped wave rolled smoothly over the thirsty sand. A gentle breeze brushed passed his face, bringing with it the tantalizing smell of a living sea. Behind him, palm trees lay silhouetted majestically against the evening sky. True, he had produced films of a supposed tropical paradise or two, but he himself had never experienced an evening to equal the serenity of this one. It was nearly perfect. If only there had been a second chair at the table. A chair just for Lori. But of course, that was impossible. Lori belonged to Brad Douglas.

Howard had to laugh as the thought came to him. How many evenings had Brad spent on this very beach dreaming of Lori? Funny how what goes around comes around. It had been Howard himself, whose actions had put Brad on this island for those ten long years. Now, it was Howard's turn to pay the piper. Oh well, there was nothing he could do to change any of that now. And so, he dined. And he enjoyed.

"Thank you, Jason Hackett," he whispered to the night. "Thank you.

CHAPTER 20

The officiator's words came to Jenice's ears like music from a symphony orchestra, and she knew this was the moment she was born for. The warmth of Michael's hand in hers sent a shiver of excitement to the depths of her heart, and she could only gaze with wonder into those piercingly tender blue eyes. She drew in an excited breath and pondered the reality of what was happening. Moments ago, she had come to the man she loved as Jenice Anderson. Moments from now, she would be kissing the man she loved as Jenice Allen, and their destinies would be forever linked.

Jenice glanced around the room at all the friends and family who had come to share the wonderful occasion. They were all there, just as she and Michael had wanted. There was Samantha's good friend Arline, whose warm smile encouraged Jenice. Beside her stood her handsome husband, Bruce Vincent, Samantha's former fiancé. He wasn't as handsome as Michael, naturally, but he was very handsome, nevertheless. Judging from the looks on Shannon and Tom's faces, she surmised that their day in the spotlight wasn't far behind. The pride in Michael's parents' eyes couldn't have been more radiant. Turning her attention to her own parents, Jenice couldn't keep the tears from flowing. For the first time in her life, Jenice understood why her mother gave up some of her most cherished dreams to marry her father. And for the first time she understood how the love they shared dwarfed any adventure her mother might have sacrificed.

A smile crossed Jenice's lips as she thought about two more names that could be added to the list of well wishers. Though they couldn't be seen, she knew in her heart that both Samantha and Jason were there. And she was glad.

Jenice's thoughts were interrupted as she heard the officiator say, "You may now kiss as man and wife." She looked again into Michael's eyes and melted in his arms as he pulled her into the most waited-for kiss of her life. And the world stood still.

EPILOGUE

"What a fitting place to come on our honeymoon," Jenice laughed, holding her face up to feel the impact of the gentle rain against her skin. "The very spot where you first proposed to me. And what a wonderful bonus this rain is. It's almost like heaven is giving me a second chance to stand here with you like this." She sighed happily. "The last time you stood in front of the Eiffel Tower in a falling rain, I was off chasing after a rainbow in another part of the world, remember?"

"How could I ever forget?" Michael agreed softly. "That was probably the unhappiest day of my life. But, my pretty little reporter, today more than makes up for it."

"Hey!" she said, suddenly inspired by an idea. "What do you say we spend every anniversary right here in Paris? I think that would be a great tradition."

"Okay by me," he quickly agreed. "But I can't guarantee rain the next time."

Jenice put her arm through Michael's and pulled him close to her. "What about the gold?" she asked. "Do we go back after it, or do we let it stay there?"

"Who cares?" Michael shrugged. "With an adventure-loving reporter like you and an adventure-loving artist like me, what do you say we just follow whatever adventure waits around the corner and let the pieces fall where they may? One of these days we may run into a situation where the gold could be useful. There'll be plenty of time to go after it if and when that happens. For now, I vote to leave it right where it's lain for the past three hundred years."

"Ya got my vote, big guy," Jenice said with a brisk nod. She turned her face upward again, studying the magnificent structure towering above them. "You know what?" she declared. "I've never climbed that thing. Have you?"

"No," he admitted. "I haven't."

Taking Michael's hand in her own, she looked again at the tower. "What do you say, Michael Allen? Shall we climb the darn thing?"

"Yeah, Jenice Allen. Let's do it."

"Jenice Allen," she smiled. "Do you have any idea how good that name sounds to me?"

Michael reached out and ran a hand through her hair. "About as good as it sounds to me," he said. Then, after pulling her into a tender kiss, he added, "Come on, let's go climb a tower."

P.S. Samantha and Jason did return to finish their tour of the exotic universe. This time, they stayed for the full two weeks. A wonderful time was had by both. And that be the truth, lads and lassies. Ye has me word on it.

ABOUT THE AUTHOR

Dan Yates has always loved being thought of as one who spins an interesting tale. Retired now, he can look back at a career that includes some fifteen years as a professional classroom instructor. "My favorite teaching tool," says Dan, "has always been a good story. Once you get someone's attention with a good story, you've left them wide open to be taught."

Dan continues to say he learned this principles from the greatest teacher who ever lived. "I never mention that teacher's name in any of my stories," Dan explains. "But this doesn't mean He isn't there. He sits in the presiding chair of the group of higher authorities often spoken of in my stories."

Dan adds that having his stories published and made available for so many to read "is one of the most humbling and one of the most exciting things ever to happen to me. I'd like to thank Covenant Communications, and especially my editor, Valerie Holladay, for all their help in make this possible."

Dan's previous writing efforts have resulted in Church productions and local publications as well as six previous best-selling novels in the *Angel* series: *Angels Don't Knock, Just Call Me an Angel, Angels to the Rescue, An Angel in the Family, It Takes an Angel* and *An Angel's Christmas.*

A former bishop and high councilor, Dan now lives in Phoenix with his wife, Shelby Jean. They have six children and nineteen grandchildren.

He still loves hearing from his readers, who have contacted him from such distant places as Hong Kong, Holland, and the Ukraine. He can be reached at **yates@swlink.net**.